THE LAST FREE MAN

AND OTHER STORIES

LEWIS WOOLSTON

TRUTH SERUM PRESS

BP#00083

Truth Serum Press
32 Meredith Street
Sefton Park SA 5083
Australia

Email: truthserumpress@live.com.au
Website: http://truthserumpress.net
Truth Serum Press catalogue:
http://truthserumpress.net/catalogue/

Cover design © Matt Potter
Front cover and back cover images © Sam Curry
Author photograph © Linsey Berryman

ISBN: 978-1-925536-88-1

Also available as an eBook
ISBN: 978-1-925536-89-8

Truth Serum Press is a member of the
Bequem Publishing collective

http://www.bequempublishing.com/

Dedicated to the memory
of my friend
Matthew Fitzgerald.

Drifter, dreamer, poet, artist,
coffee enthusiast and
boarding house raconteur.

For teaching that life
is about relationships and
experiences, adventures,
friends and lovers;
not careers and
money and houses and
investment portfolios.

He loved a good yarn over a cuppa.

Sorry he isn't here to read these stories.

CONTENTS

THE LAST FREE MAN

I met Jimmy Healy when I worked at Madura Roadhouse several years ago. He's dead now so I feel I can tell this story without upsetting anyone or causing unwanted legal grief. Jimmy was one of that dying breed of old bushies who'd been out on the Nullarbor for as long as anyone could remember. There aren't many like him anymore, the old bushmen have died, and the modern corporate world doesn't tolerate people like that.

Jimmy was known to everyone on the highway from Ceduna to Norseman as 'Jimmy Rabbit' due to being a former rabbit trapper, before the federal government wiped that trade out with the advent of Calicivirus. As I grew to know him I pieced together other parts of his story. He'd worked on every sheep station from Nundroo to Rawlinna; he'd worked on the railway line briefly, at a couple of mine sites further north of Kalgoorlie; and now in his declining old age he was with us at the Madura Roadhouse. He had also been to Vietnam, in fact he was one of the last Australian troops to leave in 1972 and this experience defined his outlook on life as I found out.

After he came back he told his fiancée he didn't want to marry her anymore, he told his family and his employer he was done with his life in the suburbs, sold or binned the bulk of his possessions and packed what was left into his old ute and headed out to the Nullarbor where he had lived and worked ever since. He was a good worker and never caused trouble despite being a bit off-tap and anti-social, so he never had a problem with finding work. There was always another sheep station, another mining camp, another roadhouse for him.

When I met him he was old, but you could still see how strong he was, muscles like rope practically popped out of every limb covered by skin that the outback sun had tanned like leather. He was easy enough to get along with so long as you weren't a 'noisy cunt' around him. Jimmy's pet hate was noisy cunts, people who insisted on talking all the time, and for this reason he spent most of his time at the roadhouse in the kitchen. He couldn't stand the grey nomads, blathering old fools making idle chit chat about the weather and asking how long had we been out here? Did we like it out here?

Jimmy would often disappear for a couple of days and go camping and shooting out on the plains, miles from anywhere. He was always happiest out there and would return refreshed and better able to tolerate the human race for a little while. I earned his trust over time by keeping to myself and not being a noisy cunt, so Jimmy took me out with him a couple of times. It was an educational experience to say the least. I had fancied myself an experienced camper who knew a bit about the bush but compared to Jimmy I was just another idiot from the city bumbling around.

I'd known him about a year when he told the boss at the roadhouse that he was quitting, retiring in fact, due to ill health. He offered me his 4WD for a very reasonable price and I agreed to drive him to Penong where he was going to live out his golden years. I took a week off and Jimmy and I headed north towards the railway line then west across the South Australian border along a track that wasn't marked on any map and was barely visible to anyone but Jimmy.

After the second day in the bush driving at Jimmy's directive, I asked him where we were going.

'To Billy Langley's grave,' he replied. I got excited. I had heard about this place before from old bushies but never known how to get there. This was real wilderness trekking.

Billy Langley's grave is known to maybe fifty people in the whole world and maybe thirty of them have actually seen it. It would have to be the loneliest grave in Australia if not the world. Not much is known about Billy Langley. It is presumed he worked on a sheep station or perhaps he was a rabbit trapper back in the day. It is known that he died on one of the most remote parts of the Nullarbor and most accounts say it was a snake bite that ended his life. We know that a mate he worked with buried him out on that desolate plain, carefully piling rocks over the grave so dingoes wouldn't dig him up. At some point he came back with a roughly hewn chunk of Nullarbor limestone and with a cold chisel he carved these words

Billy Langley
Died June 1910
Aged 35
With Jesus Now

In childlike block letters testifying to the author's semi-literate state, it stands there to this day. Unvisited by all except the few intrepid bushies who occasionally make it out this way and the Kestrels who patrol the skies above. It is hundreds of kilometres from the nearest sealed road, nearly a thousand kilometres from the nearest town and most of Australia isn't aware of its existence.

Yet amongst those who know about the grave it exerts a strange fascination. I've heard more than one old bushie tell me he'd like to be buried in the same fashion when his time comes. I can't deny that I find the idea romantic, sort of like Edgar Allen Poe meets Slim Dusty out in the middle of nowhere.

We made camp about a hundred metres from the grave out of respect and once we'd finished setting up Jimmy walked me over to see it. In and of itself it wasn't an impressive sight, rocks laid flat over dirt and the limestone marker with its primitive inscription but knowing how few people have ever seen it and how isolated it was made it awe inspiring. Billy Langley had lain here for over a century and it's highly unlikely more than a hundred people had seen his grave in all that time. The wind whipped over the barren saltbush plain with no trees to impede it and crows in the distance called to each other while I stood there and thought about life and death.

'He picked a spot alright,' was Jimmy's laconic summary of the vista and I couldn't help but agree with him. The view was overwhelming to someone who has spent most of their life in cities: it would be frightening, too much emptiness for the average suburban mind to handle.

If you stood at the foot of the grave and slowly turned in a full circle you would have a completely unimpeded view of nothing. The ground is so flat you could probably put a spirit level on it, there are no trees visible, no buildings, just a great emptiness that sends shivers through your soul. I noticed Jimmy looking around as if trying to get his bearings and asked him what he was looking for.

'I buried something here back in 1973, forty paces north of this grave it was, just figuring it out, give us a minute.' He seemed to find the direction he was looking for and started carefully measuring and counting out his paces north of the site while I stood there clueless.

Seeing that he knew what he was doing I followed blindly along, baffled by what he could have buried here so long ago and why. Eventually he was satisfied with the paces counted and ground his boot into the dust as a marker.

'Be a good bloke and get the shovel and pick from the back of the truck, would you?' he asked with a greedy grin splitting his weather-beaten face. I complied without understanding and when I brought the tools back he said that I should start digging. I penetrated the dry earth of the Nullarbor while Jimmy rolled himself a cigarette and watched me.

'Should hear a ting in a minute, stop when you hear it and we'll have a look,' he said as I dug a couple feet deeper and sure enough a few minutes later a metallic ting rang out as the pick hit something. Jimmy walked over and told me to brush off the dirt and get out of the way so he could see.

I saw the green metallic lid of some sort of box or chest, quite large, still half obscured by dust. I scratched off more dirt, and some writing became visible. It was a military label, this was some sort of army equipment. It hit me that in 1973 Jimmy was fresh out of the Army and back from Vietnam. He must have stolen something and hid it out here.

I had no time to think what it might be because Jimmy was leveraging it out of the dirt with a shovel. I helped and between the two of us we got it up and out of the hole I'd dug. Jimmy quickly loosened some latches and opened it. There were layers of plastic protecting whatever was inside and I still couldn't see it, but Jimmy gave a satisfied huff, so I gathered his primitive plastic protection had worked. He peeled layers of it back and revealed a genuine Vietnam-era Australian Army SLR resting on boxes of ammunition.

'Shit Jimmy, you've had this hidden out here since 1973? This is all kinds of illegal, plenty of people would pay good money for it though, does it still work?'

'I didn't steal it for the money, I took it to stick one up the system and I thought I might have a use for it one day. These old things were designed to be neglected and abused by arse ignorant soldiers so it's a good chance it still works, no water has got through the plastic. Put it to one side and dig a little deeper in the hole.'

I did as I was bid and a few moments later I hit another green metal chest identical to the first one. We went through the same process of leveraging it out of the hole and unwrapping layers of plastic. This time an old-school Soviet AK-47 was revealed with a few spare magazines of ammunition. Jimmy pulled it out and had a look at it while he lit another cigarette.

'Shot a Viet Cong about a month before we came back, took this off him and managed to smuggle it back to Australia then hide it out here. The Russians were giving them to the Vietnamese at the time, see that writing on the metal? That's Russian, these things are worth big money to the right people, I don't have much ammo for it though.'

I stared at the weapon in my hand, preserved in mint condition thanks to Jimmy's foresight and the layers of plastic, and wondered about the journey it had taken to reach this day. Made in some Soviet factory in the 60s, shipped to North Vietnam then smuggled south along the famous Ho Chi Minh trail where some young Viet Cong conscript carried it until he was shot down by a young Australian conscript named Jimmy Healy. He'd taken it as a souvenir of the war and hidden it out here for all those years.

My mind boggled as I stood there like a stunned mullet until Jimmy told me to stop being clueless and bring both chests to our camp. We trudged back past Billy Langley's grave to our campsite and Jimmy sat down and started cleaning both guns with oil and cotton. Muttering to himself as he performed the task, he seemed to grow more and more optimistic that they would work as he continued.

At length he stood again and loaded a magazine into the SLR, and advising me to 'mind your fucken ears mate,' he took aim at a shrub about three hundred metres to our west and fired. The noise split the silence of the saltbush plain with heartless violence, birds scattered, and I felt actual pain in my ears that travelled down my spine and rattled my balls like some great industrial violation. Jimmy's aim was spot on, the shrub exploded in a thud of dust and leaves as he fired round after round into it. I watched his face, screwed up in concentration as he took aim and fired. There was something dangerous and violent there, the killer instinct, man's inner hunter, call it what you want but I saw another side of Jimmy that day.

After maybe a dozen shots fired he asked me if I wanted to have a go and fearing being mocked for being a sook, I accepted the offered rifle. I got my posture and position right, a loose unsupported standing pose, aimed at the same shrub and pulled the trigger. The kick shook my spine and rattled my teeth, the noise was enough to make my ears give up for the day while the stench of cordite overwhelmed everything else. I took a few more shots so as not to appear weak in front of Jimmy but my heart wasn't in it. I'd shot plenty of rifles before, but they were all small calibre bolt action guns for hunting rabbits and foxes, not military grade assault weapons that had almost certainly been used to kill Viet Cong.

Hoping to distract from my weak performance, I asked Jimmy what he planned to do with the weapons now that he'd dug them up.

'Dunno, can't legally buy that calibre of ammo in this country so they have limited use. Might see if some bikies I know in Kalgoorlie want to buy them or maybe give them to someone who'll appreciate them.' I thought about what bikies in Kalgoorlie might use them for and decided I didn't want my prints on them. I rubbed down the weapon with my shirt sleeve while Jimmy gently mocked me for being overly scared of the police. He took the rifle from me and carefully cleaned it again before returning it to its case.

We stayed one night at that camp near Billy Langley's grave before moving east along what's left of the old Eyre Highway. We stopped briefly to shoot some camels when a mob of about forty came across our path. Jimmy took the right flank and I took the left and we fired and moved inwards, dropping the beasts before they could get away. We left the carcasses where they fell because in Jimmy's opinion, 'Dingoes need to eat same as you and me and if they get a taste for camel they might bring a few down themselves.'

We crossed over the modern highway like it was Checkpoint Charlie letting us back into civilization. We soon got off it again and set up camp right next to the cliff edge, maybe fifty kms west of Nullarbor Roadhouse. The stars that night were spectacular, it seemed like you could reach your hand into the sky and pull down a galaxy, and so long as I live I want to remember that night. We could hear but not see the ocean as it crashed against the limestone cliffs. We could just see and hear the trucks driving through the night on the highway, their lights on high beam penetrating the desert darkness.

It was while I was contemplating all this that Jimmy told me he was dying.

He'd had a 'mob of tests done' by the doctor in Kalgoorlie and the diagnosis was terminal, he had been told maybe eighteen months to live at the most but he himself thought a year more likely as he had no intention of going to a hospital to die. His plan was to live in Penong by himself in a house he would rent from a bloke he knew and when he got too sick to live independently, he would end his life with his own hand. He told me the blackfellas had taught him all about the plants on the

Nullarbor and he had stockpiled some seeds which would give him a quick painless death when the time came.

At times like this I am basically useless, worse than useless in fact; I never know the appropriate thing to say or do. Instead I become an awkward twit who ends up saying something stupid or insensitive. Fortunately, Jimmy spared me the agony of embarrassing myself by launching into the longest speech I had ever heard from a man normally so silent and to the point. His speech went on for some time with only brief pauses for cigarettes and I listened without interrupting, sensing that this would be one of the most important things I would ever hear in my life, something I would remember for a long time.

'It's a fucken waste of time complaining about dying, every living thing dies so why should you be special? People get so attached to the idea that they are different from everything in nature that they are legit shocked when natural things like death happen to them.'

'I've had a good life but more importantly I've cheated the system, I wasn't supposed to have this life out here in the bush, being free. I was supposed to be a tradie in the suburbs, married with kids, nice house on a nice street and all that shit. Getting the nasho call up and going to Vietnam changed everything. I saw what it's all really about over there. See, before I got sent over there I actually believed in the dream. I legit thought that having a steady job, a missus and kids, paying off your mortgage and saving for retirement was the way to go. Then I saw what the system really was. Us poor cunts that got called up to be nashos, we were just toys and tools for the system to use, then when we got back we were expected to be good little workers again like nothing had happened.'

'But something did happen, and I couldn't go back to the way things were. Originally I only meant to come out here for a few months and get my head clear again before I worked out what I was going to do with my life. Thing is I worked out I could be free out here, or at least a lot freer than I could in the city and after the regimented life in the army I wanted freedom more than I wanted a normal life.'

'That's it really, I made a choice between freedom and a normal life. Now I'm almost ready to leave the stage so to speak I can look back and I reckon I made the right choice. It's better to be free than normal.'

'I never told anyone this at the time but about a year ago the woman I was supposed to marry came through the roadhouse. Her name was Catherine, we were engaged before I got the nasho call up. After I came back from Vietnam I told her I wasn't going to marry her. She did all the tears and drama stuff, all the bullshit that women do to suck you in, but I stayed firm and left. Never saw her again until a year ago. She had found another bloke to marry, almost exactly like I was back in the day, steady job, decent trade, totally normal in every way. She had obviously forgotten all about me because she never recognized me at all. Just came in and paid for fuel, made the usual chit chat and off they went.'

'I saw her husband, the bloke she found to replace me after I done a bunk. He was so worn out and dominated by her I felt sorry for him. Not a scrap of jealousy anymore, just pity for the poor bastard having spent his life slaving away to house and feed that woman and however many brats she shat out. Having to listen to her blather every day, never being free in all those years and now he's old and worn out so he'll die trapped.'

'I escaped that life but only because national service and Vietnam woke me up. If that hadn't happened I would have been exactly like him. It scares me to think how close I came.'

'I could have been that henpecked old man wearing socks and sandals and doing the grey nomad thing around the country. Instead I'm free, I've lived a really amazing life out here. I've seen things that most people will never see, things that most people don't even know exist. Most importantly I've managed to not answer to anyone for most of my life. I've never had to stay in a job I hate because I have kids to feed or a mortgage to pay. That's not nothing young fella.'

'What you realize if you see a bit of life and pay attention is that misery and unhappiness is actually the norm for human life. The majority of the population of the world lives in third world shitholes where they are starving or being bombed or raped by soldiers or whatever but even in first world countries like Australia misery is normal. Most people in this country will be wage slaves their entire life, constantly worried about how they're going to pay the bills, frightened of losing their jobs, arguing with the missus and all that shit. They will live unhappy and die unhappy and their children will carry on their unhappiness after they die. When we think of people achieving something big we think of self-made millionaires or movie stars but merely escaping the crushing drudgery and misery that everyone else is in is a huge achievement. I've done that, nobody will write a book about me or make a movie of my life, but my life has been remarkable.'

With that he finished his cigarette and settled himself into his swag for the night. I lay awake for hours listening to the ocean crash against the cliffs and the occasional road train thinking about all he had said. I remember looking up at the stars and realizing he was right on every important point that he'd said. I knew then that I was going to chart my life on a different course thanks to Jimmy.

In the morning we cooked bacon and eggs on our little fire as the sun slowly rose and illuminated the Great Australian Bight. The ocean changed colours with the sun and the terns nesting in the cliffs started their morning hunt for fish. I ate my bacon and eggs with some bread and looked out on the Southern Ocean thinking of how many miles of marine wilderness lay between me and Antarctica at that exact moment.

We packed up and returned to the highway, civilization re-entered our lives in the form of shitbox vans driven incompetently by European backpackers and expensive caravans also driven incompetently by grey nomads. Jimmy navigated his way around them without losing his temper as we headed towards Penong.

When we arrived in Penong we made directly for the house Jimmy was going to live out the rest of his days in. It was a humble place, at least fifty years old and a little weather-beaten but comfortable enough. It was on the eastern edge of the small town and had a brilliant view of the wheat and sheep farms that stretched off into the distance as well as the highway and the local cemetery. Jimmy shifted what little gear he had into the house, for a man of his age he had not accumulated many possessions and everything he owned in the world took the two of us three trips to bring in from his vehicle.

Jimmy gave me some cash and told me to walk up to the local pub and get us a 'carton of something decent to drink' while he sorted out his stuff. I obeyed and walked through the tiny town listening to the sounds of Magpies warbling, Willy Wagtails and kids playing backyard cricket and thought to myself that this wasn't such a bad place to live out your final year of life.

When I came back with the carton Jimmy was squared away and rolling a cigarette on the front porch. We both opened a stubby and sat down to take in the view. After a few moments Jimmy pointed out the cemetery.

'I'm going to use the money I've saved to get myself a plot down there, organize everything before the time comes. It's not a bad spot I reckon. I was just watching and there are a pair of Kestrels nesting in the tree by the cemetery fence. I like the idea of having Kestrels living by my grave. Free birds looking over the grave of a free man. Fucking poetic and all that.'

He smiled and I felt very happy for reasons I couldn't quite explain. Jimmy had shown me how to live and what really mattered in life. I left the next day and drove back to the roadhouse. I never saw Jimmy alive again and he died by his own hand about eleven months later, just as the pain was becoming intolerable. He kept his freedom to the very end and that is not nothing.

I still visit his grave there in the Penong cemetery every time I travel through. The Kestrels are still nesting in that tree by the fence line. Free birds looking over the grave of a free man.

THE LAST MADURA BRUMBY

Madura didn't start off as a roadhouse. When the first white people settled in the area there was no highway nor had cars been invented.

It was originally established as a horse breeding station in the 1870s. They bred and exported horses for the British Army in India. Queen Victoria's colonial garrisons had an insatiable need for horseflesh, so it was a profitable trade for many years, despite the hardships of living and working in such a remote place.

The horses were raised on the wide saltbush plain to the south of where the highway is now. When they were ready for duty in Her Majesty's colonial forces they were mustered up to Eucla and put on a ship to India. I can't help thinking it would have been a sad experience for a horse that was half wild on the Nullarbor to be shipped to India where it would have laboured long and hard and would probably die horribly in battle or from thirst, heat or disease. The enlisted troopers who rode the horses were probably the dregs of the British working class who joined the Army to escape Dickensian slums. At least the horses had once known freedom.

Right from the start there were some horses that escaped and went wild. Most, of course, died but a few tough ones survived and formed the first Brumby herds in Western Australia. These herds became a common sight to people who travelled the remote parts of the country.

The Army horse trade boomed during the First World War then died a slow lingering death before finally shutting down in the 1930s when the station converted to sheep. Herds of wild Brumbies were a common sight in the district right up until the early 1960s. When the highway was finally sealed in the late '60s and early '70s the old homestead was abandoned, and the current roadhouse was built. The Nullarbor became a place of tourists and truckies and Brumbies had no place in the modern world.

The Brumby herds in the area soon learned to stay away from the new sealed highway and most of them stuck to the north of it. Bushies who went on rabbit shooting trips off the beaten track still regularly reported seeing Brumby herds of thirty or forty animals running wild. Most bushies wouldn't shoot a Brumby out of some unspoken respect they felt for the creatures.

The last big herds were seen in the late '80s and early '90s in the north towards the railway line. A worker at the railway camp at Forrest reported seeing a herd of twenty Brumbies taking turns to drink from a puddle created by a water tank leak at the camp in 1993. That was probably the last of the big herds in the area.

By the time I got to Madura in 2013 it was basically assumed that the days of Brumbies were over. Some of the older bushies I met could remember seeing them twenty years earlier, but the most recent credible sighting was of a sickly-looking pair north of Mundrabilla in 2001.

Jimmy Healy was still alive in those days and he spotted what I believe to be the last wild Brumby of the Nullarbor. It was mostly luck he spotted it and he saw it on the south side of the highway near the coast, the exact opposite of where everyone else looked for them.

He told me about it and commanded me to keep my mouth shut before he took me to the spot. We followed the rough dirt track that rambled to the coast. Only a dozen or so very keen fishermen used this track every year, so we were totally alone. We swung off to the east along what remained of the old Telegraph Road. Most of the track had been covered by vegetation or creeping sand dunes and it was obvious no one had been down here for years. We startled a mob of emus and they ran before us like prehistoric relics.

Jimmy parked the car in the scrub and we walked to the small waterhole where he'd seen the animal. The waterhole was basically a puddle in the sand which held its water most of the year thanks to its sheltered position in the lee of a huge sand dune. All the animals for miles around came here and the ground was covered in tracks. Jimmy had his head down looking for horse tracks. He found them in a couple of minutes and pointed them out to me.

'She's walking slowly, she looked pretty old and worn out when I saw her. Not long for this world I reckon.'

'How do you know it's a she?'

'Saw it close enough to know, it's a mare and an old one, she's probably had a hard life out here and now she's all alone just waiting to die.'

I quietly digested this info while Jimmy looked around at the tracks on the ground. What must her life be like living alone as the last of its herd in the middle of nowhere? Did wild horses get lonely? I'd heard once that dogs would curl up and die if left alone for too long, apparently their pack instinct is so strong they can't survive without company; perhaps it was the same for horses.

Jimmy interrupted my thoughts by telling me to get in the car. He said we'd be best off getting to higher ground and having a look over the plain.

With great difficulty we inched the car to the top of a sand dune and parked it there. From that position I could look south and see the Great Southern Ocean stretching unbroken to Antarctica or I could look north and see the vast saltbush plain that made up the interior of Australia. The plains around the Madura area follow a very simple and uniform pattern. They stretch south of the highway, miles and miles of open, flat saltbush with occasional clumps of mulga trees, before meeting a band of huge sand dunes that form a buffer between the plain and the beach. The sand dunes give a little shelter from the wind and small waterholes sometimes form in their lee. This is often the best place to look for animals.

We got out of the car and stood awkwardly on the loose sand of the dune. Despite being older than me Jimmy's eyes were keener, and he spotted the horse first. I had trouble locating it on the vast empty plain even after he pointed it out to me. It was a sorry looking creature, dusty brown and bedraggled, moping as it plodded along through the dust. I couldn't help but think of that cartoon donkey from Winnie the Pooh.

'She's a sad old girl.' Jimmy's laconic comment summed up the picture perfectly. The old mare looked ready to die. As if life had become an intolerable burden for her. She slowly made her way to the water and slopped at the muddy puddle like a bedridden old person being spoon-fed in their hospital bed.

'Wouldn't it be kinder to shoot her?' I asked and got an angry glare from Jimmy for my trouble.

'You shoot her and I'll shoot you.'

I said nothing in order to not provoke his anger further. We watched the old horse for a while and when it had finished drinking and retired to the nearest clump of scrub we got in the car and headed off. I never saw it again and Jimmy himself died a year or so later. I've never heard of anyone seeing any Brumbies in the Madura area since that time. It seems a safe bet that I saw the last Madura Brumby.

WINTER IN NORSEMAN

He arrived in town on the very last day of March. Norseman was familiar with new arrivals and blow-ins coming to work in the mines so no one made very much fuss about it. He rented an old weatherboard house one street off the highway with a yard that hadn't been maintained since who knew when. His landlord noted that he didn't seem to have much gear to shift in but he didn't care enough to ask about it. The mines had slowed down a bit in the last eighteen months or so and paying tenants had been hard to find so there was an incentive to not ask questions if his money was good.

He quickly found a job at the local bottleshop, a hideous construction loosely attached to the side of the local pub; it looked like a drive through dog cage with beer ads plastered all over it. His boss owned both the bottleshop and the pub it was attached to, he soon decided this newcomer was alright, he showed up to work on time and sober and didn't steal and that was more than half the dropkicks he'd had working for him over the years could manage.

He got into a routine quickly, five or six shifts at the bottleshop each week depending on who else had left and whether or not a replacement had been found. He lived frugally and his diet was classic bachelor material, ham and cheese toasties and tinned spaghetti. His only small extravagance was the occasional science fiction novel ordered over the internet and delivered via the small local post office. He kept to himself and didn't participate in the social life of the town.

He got to know the bottleshop regulars, functional and not so functional alcoholics in various states of decline, young ones trying to escape the boredom of small-town life with sugary pre-mixed muck and the social people in town always buying a carton on the weekend for whatever barbeque or footy function they had going.

The boss had told him on the first day that 'You'll meet Tommy soon enough,' as if it were some grim prophecy. According to the boss, Tommy was the town drunk and 'a useless sack of shit' who had a habit of pissing and vomiting in public whenever the need arose.

The other staff at the pub gave their opinions on Tommy. Some said he was a Vietnam veteran, that he had been at the battle of Long Tan and the reason he was a hopeless alcoholic was due to the trauma of Vietnam. Others pointed out that Tommy wasn't old enough to have been in the Vietnam War. They favored the theory that Tommy was an old lag who'd done twenty or thirty years in prison and was now drinking away the remains of a wasted life. Nobody had any evidence to back up any of these theories but that didn't stop them discussing them.

For the first week or so the newcomer passively watched as Tommy waddled into the bottleshop first thing every morning, hands held against his body to try and hide the shakes. He watched as Tommy seemed to psych himself up for the attempt at getting his bottle off the shelf. He saw the way Tommy made a cradle in his arms for the bottle rather than holding it in his hands normally because his shakes made that too difficult.

The newcomer saw all this and took pity on poor old Tommy. He started placing a bottle of Tommy's preferred swill on the counter first thing in the morning. Tommy would walk in and he would nod in the direction of the counter not needing to say anything. Tommy was grateful in the way only the truly pathetic can be.

'You're a top bloke, I'll tell your boss how tops you are, you should be running the joint! Looking after an old bloke like me, still decent people in the world, just got to find 'em, I reckon.' And so on until he started the daily struggle to handle his meager cash without dropping it and embarrassing himself. Here again the newcomer took a step of practical compassion, holding his own hands out, cupped to receive the mess of coins Tommy was drawing with great effort out of his pocket. He would count it out and give back any change in a small plastic coin bag for Tommy's convenience.

Desperate to get back home and imbibe his medicine Tommy would nonetheless tell him what a top bloke he was and wish him a good day.

'Take her easy old mate,' was all the newcomer would say but to a man like Tommy, starved of human affection and dignity, it was like water in the desert. He would scuttle off to his filthy fibro granny flat near the railway line with a sense of warmth and belonging. The newcomer didn't know it but he had won a staunch friend.

April stretched into May which turned into June as the weather grew cold and miserable. The routine of life in Norseman went on much as it always has. There wasn't that much to the town, four streets and a couple of big truck stops for passing traffic. Most people driving through saw the truck stops and never realized there was a town attached. They didn't miss much. Nothing exciting ever happened. The newcomer started rugging up more at night and wore a jumper to work but the day to day tasks at the bottleshop remained the same.

Tommy got into trouble again for pissing on the footpath out the front of the Post Office while drunk. The local police took him in and let him sleep it off in a cell for 48 hours without much fuss. The formalities of police process that might have been stringently adhered to in the city were often waived in the bush. A local copper worth his salt knows when it's pointless to formally charge someone and Tommy was a waste of effort in anyone's book.

When Tommy was sobered up the Sergeant gave him a sandwich and asked how he was. He got a non-committal grunt in reply and before he could say anything the phone rang. He went to answer it leaving the cell door open, Tommy was no danger to anyone so the normal security procedures were ignored. Tommy sat quietly and nibbled at his sandwich, listening in to the Sergeant's phone call. He heard the newcomer's name mentioned and became curious.

'Yeah, he's been in town about four months I think, never caused any trouble, works at the bottleshop, keeps to himself. Victorian warrant? What for? Shit, so you'll be wanting him then? You're gonna send a bloke all the way from Melbourne for him? We could always pick him up and hold him until he gets here. Why not? Fine, do it your way then, you want us to pick up your bloke from Kal airport? Fine, do it your way then. Tell him to drop into the station when he gets here.' The Sergeant was annoyed at being talked down to by some detective in Melbourne who obviously thought his shit didn't stink. Country people often get bristly about being looked down upon by city people and take it very personally. City people are mostly oblivious to the offence they cause.

Tommy listened and absorbed this conversation, turned it round in his mind while he waited to be let go. He was undecided what, if anything, he would do until the Sergeant released him.

'Off you go till next time Tommy, try staying home when you drink, least that way if you piss on the ground no one cares.' The light hearted, almost good-natured contempt the Sergeant had for Tommy and his alcoholic escapades were what decided him. Tommy was a beaten dog but even beaten dogs have their pride and if pushed beyond a certain point will bite back.

Tommy rushed to the newcomer's house and knocked on the door. In a small town like Norseman everyone knows where everyone else lives especially the town drunk. The newcomer answered the door in his trakky daks and an old t-shirt. A surprised look crossed his face to see Tommy outside of the bottleshop.

Tommy blurted out the conversation he had overheard in a jumbled rush.

'I think you'd best come in bloke,' the newcomer said and Tommy almost cried. It had been at least twenty years since anyone had invited him into their house. For a moment he felt like a human again.

Tommy shuffled inside meekly, the newcomer telling him to sit down on the old secondhand couch which wasn't his but had been here when he moved in. As Tommy sat down gingerly, as if expecting it all to be an elaborate prank, the newcomer asked if he wanted a coffee with some Baileys in it. Tommy smiled and asked if the Pope was Catholic and a bond of trust was established.

Sipping his coffee with Baileys Tommy slowly and carefully repeated the conversation he had overheard the Sergeant having on the phone. The newcomer grimaced. He knew exactly what this meant and he would have to act now.

'I appreciate you telling me this mate, I'll have to leave town but at least I'll have a head start on them, any reason you're giving me warning? Not everyone would.' Tommy thought about the question for a second. Being a man of few words and little education and weighed down by years of hard drinking he struggled to express himself. When they came the words burst out in a bitter eruption.

'They've always shit on me, everyone in this town, I see the way they look at me and talk about me when they think I'm not listening. Fuck them. You were decent to me, so I'd rather help you out especially if it sticks a rocket up their arses.' The newcomer nodded and the two men smiled at each other in understanding, the fellowship of beaten dogs who've been shat on by life. Composing himself by taking a deep breath, the newcomer told Tommy he'd have to pack up and go if he wanted to be far enough away before the Victorian detective got here. He gave Tommy the rest of the bottle of Baileys to take home with him and they parted friends.

Tommy walked home feeling virtuous, as if he'd done some great and noble deed which would set the world to rights and be spoken of for years to come. He sipped the Baileys and sang an old Rod Stewart song as he trudged along.

Two days later the Victorian detective arrived and immediately annoyed the Sergeant. Despite understanding and usually obeying the rank structure of the police force, the Sergeant didn't like being spoken down to. Add to this the ingrained disdain that country people have for city people who think they're better and the two were at loggerheads.

The Victorian detective was eager to bag his quarry, so they headed around to the newcomer's house. They spent five minutes or so knocking on the door and looking through the windows before admitting he was probably gone. The Sergeant sent a constable around to the landlord's house and he returned with a key; they entered and found the place deserted, cleaned up and empty.

'Reckon he got wind of you coming mate, looks like he's done the bolt,' the Sergeant taunted the Victorian detective. He was quietly glad to have got one over on this ponce from the city who thought he was such hot shit. He didn't really care about what the newcomer may or may not have done in Melbourne twelve months ago. He'd caused no trouble here in Norseman and that was the limit of the Sergeant's cares.

They looked through the small fibro house and other than a toasted sandwich maker and a pile of science fiction novels he'd obviously finished, the newcomer had left nothing behind. The

Victorian detective knelt and looked through the books with their lurid cover illustrations as if they would give him some clue of where his fugitive had disappeared to.

The Sergeant walked outside and in hushed tones shared his pleasure with the constable.

'He's been tipped off somehow and gone, maybe a day or two ago, could be halfway across the country by now. This fuckwit thinks he's Sherlock Holmes or something, if the bloke is smart enough to not get caught for twelve months that the warrant's been out on him then he's smart enough to not get caught for a long time yet. They've got Buckley's and they know it but they think they're so much better than us so they won't admit it.' The young constable nodded, absorbing the wisdom of his Sergeant in this matter. Country policing is very much a learn from the elders process and this young man was coming along just fine.

At length the Victorian detective gave up his search of the house and informed the Sergeant he would be in touch with his superiors in Melbourne to get instructions on how to proceed. The Sergeant was feeling somewhat vindicated and decided to give his cage a rattle.

'Make sure you tell the head honcho over east that I offered to pick him up and hold him for you but you wanted me to wait until you got here. Important detail they'll want to hear, I reckon.' The Victorian detective gave him a furious glare and stormed off while the Sergeant basked in the admiration of the young constable.

'Now that, my boy, is how you deal with fuckwits from the city.'

The Sergeant was very pleased with himself. He didn't really care about crimes in Melbourne, this bloke probably wasn't the first shitbag on the run to come through Norseman and he was unlikely to be the last either. So long as they behaved themselves in his town, all was right with the Sergeant's world.

They went to the patrol car, it was nearly lunch time and the Sergeant fancied going down to the servo for a pie. The young constable put his hand on the door handle and felt wet warmth. He looked closer, sniffed his hand and realized someone had pissed on the door of the car, presumably while they were inside talking to the Victorian detective.

'Sarge, look at this,' he said but the Sergeant had already noticed and was looking around for the culprit. Sure enough there was Tommy shuffling off down the street, three-quarters pissed and chuckling to himself like an idiot.

POSTCARD FROM CAIRNS

I'd moved to Alice Springs because I felt I needed to settle down for a while. I'd been living and working in the bush for five years. All the time spent in the middle of nowhere had left me disconnected from society. I decided to give it six months regardless of how I felt.

I had thought of moving back to the city but couldn't see how it was going to work. Adelaide had died in the arse economically and I'd be lucky to even get part time work there. Perth was too expensive to live and too far from everything else. Alice Springs seemed like a safe bet. If at the end of the six months I decided I couldn't hack living in town, it was a simple matter to head out bush again.

I got a place just across the road from the hospital. A nice little fenced off complex of units where everyone was from somewhere else and just here for work. Transient, anonymous and easy.

I got a job at one of the pubs in town. Two thirds of the staff were European backpackers just here for a short time. They treated the pub like a hostel, everyone was rooting someone else who worked there, travel plans were made and a lot of alcohol was drunk. Transient, anonymous and easy.

I decided to cut my rent in half by going across the road and putting a notice on the hospital's staff notice board. The place was full of nurses who were on short contracts and needed a place to live. They came here from the cities back east because the money was better and being able to put some stuff about indigenous health on their resumé helped their career no end. During their time in Alice Springs they partied with other nurses and doctors, avoided the locals like the plague and sometimes managed to get a ring on their finger or a dose of the clap. Transient, anonymous and easy.

The nurse who rang me first was named Melinda. She was from somewhere on the Central Coast of NSW, Gosford I think, she had that classic surfie bum hair that got blonder as it got longer. I showed her the spare room and told her the price and she was up for it. She moved in right away and we got comfortable living in the same house. I did my shifts at the pub while she did hers at the hospital. Neither of us gave a flying fuck about the town, we both understood that Alice Springs was a place to live temporarily and we had no interaction with any locals.

Occasionally she'd get together with a couple of the other nurses and come to the pub while I was working. Because I didn't give a fuck about the job I'd slip them a free drink or two, justifying it on the grounds that drunk young women tend to attract more customers to a pub. They would get loose and loud and have a grand old time.

Inevitably I would drive them home, Melinda would sit next to me and drivel shit in my ear while I drove and the other girls would sit in the back and sing. 'Why'd you have to go and make things so complicated?' They would sing with their heads hanging out the window and we'd get stares from any pedestrians who were out. I'd tell them to chill out in my car and they'd dismiss it; 'aww, you love us' they'd say and I couldn't really deny it.

The next morning I would have three or four hung over nurses lurking around my place barely dressed. I'd make them breakfast if they thought they could hold it down and chill out with them.

Nothing ever happened between Melinda and me, nothing ever happened between me and her nurse friends either. If I had been a little sharper and tried a little harder I probably could have fucked at least one of them but I never did. I was too shy, too decent and I always opted for the quiet life rather than try for greater heights sexually.

Melinda lived with me for six months until her contract at the hospital expired. She went back to NSW with an improved resume and a bunch of new friends on Facebook of which I was only one and probably not a very important one. That's the way it goes in these places. Transient, anonymous and easy.

I needed a new housemate and one of the backpacker girls at the pub had a friend so without further ado she came and had a look at the place. Her name was Madeline and she was English. Not lower-class English either, proper posh accent, went to a posh school, the whole deal. She was doing the standard backpacker thing, working and travelling around Australia having the time of her life. She'd just spent a couple of months doing the required amount of fruit picking down in Renmark to qualify for a second year on her visa. Now she was looking for a job and a place to live here in Alice Springs.

She moved in and we got along just fine. She wasn't as much of a party animal as most of the other backpackers and we could have actual conversations about stuff. She was very interested in hearing about my years out bush and the places where I'd lived and worked. I took her out to Ormiston Gorge on my day off and showed her the sights.

We spent a lot of time together, more than housemates normally would, and I began to think there was something there. Our mutual friends began to think so as well. I was too shy and cautious to try my luck so we hovered in the no man's land of being just really good friends.

Four months went past like nothing. She began to plan the next part of her Australian adventure. She told me she would be leaving in a week and flying to Cairns and meeting friends there. They had organised to get themselves a van and drive down the east coast.

I wished her luck and thought about putting my cards on the table and telling her how I felt. I was just about to but my shyness stopped me, so I weakly told her to send me a postcard instead.

I took her to the airport on the day she left. We chatted for a bit about nothing much and when her flight was called I almost blurted out how I felt there and then but I restrained myself and without much fuss she gave me a hug and said goodbye. I went home to an empty house and drank the rest of the day away.

The routine of my life went on, I worked at the pub and bummed around the house on my days off. I thought about getting a new housemate but the lease would be up soon and I didn't feel like extending it. I made a decision to go back out bush and not bother with the civilized world for a while. I'd made an attempt, gone on record as having tried and I hadn't exactly hit it for six. Some people just aren't destined to do the settled down family life thing, I told myself, I was better off being out bush where I didn't have to try and fit in with society.

Two weeks after she left Madeline sent me a postcard from Cairns as promised. She didn't say much, she was having a good time and had met some cool people and was looking forward to the big drive down the east coast. I looked at the card for a long time, as if it was some sort of sacred relic whose mysteries I could unlock. I knew I would never see her again. She had already moved on with her life. Whatever I had wanted to say before she left would never be said. We'd had our time and that was that.

Transient, anonymous and easy.

DRIFTWOOD

I first met Helen and Louise when I was on holiday in Brisbane. They were living with my cousin Jacob in a big share house in a suburb only a few train stops from the city. Like most young people living in that sort of situation they were as poor as church mice and being cashed up from working in the bush I was over generous with my money. I would buy us all a carton of cider and order Chinese or pizza delivered to the house and insist they join in. They happily partook and cheerfully tolerated my bullshit stories about life on the Nullarbor.

Helen was thin and had a touch of blonde in her hair while Louise was curvy and brunette. Both of them had a slightly seedy air about them and I had my suspicions about drug use in their past although they seemed clean now. I felt some attraction to Helen, I've always had a thing for tall skinny girls, and I got a vibe that she felt something too.

Helen asked questions about my life out there and what the work was like. She admitted to being sick of the treadmill of wage slavery and stress in the city. I answered her questions expansively, telling her all about how easy it was to save money out there and how we were free in a way that city people can't be. They got interested but didn't seem likely to do anything about it.

I left my cousin's place and went back to work at Madura roadhouse. Upon arriving I discovered that the drunken bum who had been manager had quit just before he was going to get sacked but even worse than that several of the other staff had quit in disgust and frustration at having to work under an alcoholic clown. The owner had come up from Esperance and was holding the fort until a new manager could be found. It looked like I wouldn't be getting a day off anytime soon.

The owner told me bluntly that he would take the first person who wanted to work there, so I suggested Helen and Louise. I called my cousin Jacob and told him that if the girls were keen there was a job going; they rang back within the hour and after a quick chat to the boss they were hired and told to get here as soon as they could.

They booked the flights to Perth and the train to Kalgoorlie and I was sent to pick them up while the boss ran the roadhouse almost single-handedly. I arrived in Kalgoorlie almost an hour before the train did and idly hung around the station. I stared at the war memorial statue out front for a while; it always bothered me that the digger on top of the plinth seemed to be thrusting his bayonet at the people getting off the train. Was this Kalgoorlie's subtle way of telling outsiders to go away? My musing was interrupted by the arrival of the train.

Helen and Louise looked exhausted and frazzled so I gathered up their bags into my car and we went off to the motel for the night. I explained to them that there wasn't really much of a shop out at the roadhouse so if they wanted anything they should get it while we were here in Kalgoorlie. They spent the rest of the arvo stocking up on soap, shampoo and tampons while I raided the small bookstore in town. We ate Chinese and watched *2 Broke Girls* reruns on TV that night and then at first light the next morning we headed off towards Madura.

It was their first time in the outback; I could tell by the way their eyes boggled as we got further and further out from civilization. The wrecks and roadkill on the side of the highway made a particular impression on them. Then when we hit the 90 mile straight where the country flattens out and opens up, they struggled to deal with the sight of so much nothing. I stopped by the side of the road and let them out to take it all in, the dead straight highway, the flat treeless plain, the vast nothing; they were shocked out of their tiny suburban minds. I had a good chuckle and we got going again.

The boss got them to fill out all the usual paperwork and they got a room in the staff quarters one each side of me. Despite the initial shock they settled in well, the work wasn't a big deal and once they got the hang of the place they did just fine.

They combatted the boredom in different ways. Helen would borrow my books after I finished reading them or come to my room to watch DVDs, Louise made friends with the blokes from the nearby sheep station and was always getting invited out to go shooting or drinking with them.

After six months or so I became aware that Louise had become romantically involved with Dave; he'd been a worker on the station for several years and had only just been promoted to manager. Louise quit working at the roadhouse and moved out to the sheep station with Dave. He got her a job there but within a few months they had gone to Norseman and been married in the town hall by a JP. Apparently, Louise was pregnant.

Being somewhat socially clueless I had missed most of this until after it had already happened. Other people's love lives are not very interesting to me and I prefer to keep myself to myself. I asked Helen what she thought about it.

'She never intended to go back to the life we had in Brisbane, it was pretty shit so I can't blame her, her whole plan was to get knocked up and married to a man who could look after her. She'll do fine, Dave is alright, he's not going to bash her and there aren't any other women out there so he can't cheat on her, in six months' time she'll pretend like she's been out there forever, she'll be queen bee of that station and have everyone under her thumb. Best of luck to them both.'

I pondered her words and couldn't really disagree with her view of the situation. I've known plenty of people who were poverty-stricken nobodies in the city who came out bush, made a life for themselves and pretended they were locals, like all those years being on the bottom of the shit pile in the city never happened. Truth be told I've done it myself. I don't see what's so bad about it either. If you have the brains and balls to get out from under and make a better life for yourself, I say you've earned the right to forget the years of misery that preceded it.

Helen didn't begrudge Louise her happy outcome and neither did I. The thought occurred to me that if Louise had a plan before she came out here then maybe Helen did too. I asked her about it.

'Just to be away from all that shit and misery. I'd had a friend die from heroin just a few months before you met us. I

37

was working as a check out chick at K Mart and barely making enough to survive every week, rents in the city are retarded. Then you came along with the offer of this job, getting housed and fed by the boss as well as paid decent. Well, there was no way I was going to turn it down was I?'

I jokingly asked if she had planned to get pregnant and married as well. She laughed and said if neither of us was doing anything in a couple of years we'd shack up. I told her I would hold her to that.

Life went on for a few months and I felt the need to return to civilization for a while. I gave notice and planned to move to Adelaide. Helen sulked a little when I told her what I was doing, I got the distinct impression she was almost ready to tell me how she really felt but couldn't quite get the words out. I gave her a hug as I was leaving and she snuck a kiss that was so quick and light it could be denied with plausibility.

I enjoyed life in Adelaide for about a week then realized I'd made a mistake. The rent I had to pay for a shitbox flat was ridiculous, the job I had was uncertain and I was made very aware that I was replaceable. After the wide-open spaces of the Nullarbor the city felt cramped and dirty. I caught up with some people I'd known and they were doing the exact same thing they had been doing when I left Adelaide years ago. I realized then that this wasn't so much a city as an above ground cemetery. These people were dead, they just hadn't stopped walking around and going to work yet.

I started thinking about my return to the Nullarbor. I knew from experience that staffing was a massive problem out there so I knew I could get a job fairly easy; it was just a matter of making some calls. Before I got too far Helen called me from Ceduna and told me she would be on the REX flight tomorrow.

I waited at the airport and saw her come off the crappy little plane. When she saw me, she ran up and gave me a proper kiss. We were apparently a couple now. I drove her back to my place and we talked about what we were doing. She said she had missed me and wanted to give city life a try again. I told her that I was almost ready to pack it in and head back out to the Nullarbor but now she was here I'd hold off on that.

The flat I had was only one bedroom and I wondered what our arrangements were going to be but Helen seemed to have already decided she was my proper full-time girlfriend now and entitled to sleep with me. I fell into the couple's lifestyle with her fairly easy. Perhaps having her make the decision with minimal input from me made it easier. Whatever the case we were a good fit together, both the company and the sex was really good. We could spend all day together without annoying each other, she was content to let me read in silence on the couch and I would cook for her every evening in the tiny, mould-ridden kitchen of our flat.

She got a crappy job and started helping out with the rent so that made city life a bit more bearable. We were still pretty much living hand to mouth though and there was no sign it would get better anytime soon.

Winter kicked in with a vengeance, there are very few things more miserable than winter in Adelaide, and I found myself getting depressed and moody. On my days off I would barely leave the flat unless Helen insisted we go out and do something. I started talking about going back to the Nullarbor with her and she warmed to the idea. We started making some phone calls to people we knew out there. Helen spoke to Louise and found out she'd had the baby, a boy, and was well settled in her life as wife of the station boss.

'She's completely forgotten or refuses to remember that she was just a Bogan shitbag from Caboolture until a year and a half ago. She makes it sound like she's been a country girl all her life. She told me she's so happy to have had a son because it's the fifth generation of our family to be on the land. She actually said that bullshit 'fifth generation of our family on the land.' Her dad is an accountant in Brisbane for fuck's sake. She's married the station boss and had his baby now she talks like a country singer. Unbelievable! I felt like reminding her of all the times we got off our faces in Fortitude Valley and she went home with randoms. How quick she changes her tune.'

Helen's disgust and rage seethed out of her in an impressive fashion. I laughed a little and got a glare for my trouble.

'What does it matter? She's made the best of things and built a new life for herself, good luck to her I say. Are you jealous?'

'Yeah, I'm jealous that I'm not wifed up to a man who's covered in red dust and sheep shit every day. Jealous that I'm not stuck at a homestead in the middle of nowhere looking after a brat.'

I could see she was really bothered but wouldn't admit it. I put my arm around her and she leaned into me for comfort. We had nothing to our names but we cared for each other. The need to leave Adelaide became more urgent.

We made some more phone calls and Mundrabilla roadhouse told us we could have a spot there if we could get there right away. We quit our crappy Adelaide jobs via text message, no notice, no nothing, packed our shit and got ready to leave.

For our last night we decided to go out and do something. We went to some half-posh place on Rundle Street to eat overpriced pasta and then headed to the Crown & Anchor for drinks. It started out okay but we both found it kind of depressing. We didn't actually have any friends in Adelaide to say goodbye to, no one cared that we were leaving, our life here had made zero impact.

We ended up in the front bar of the Crown & Anchor listening to the jukebox. We sat and drank with each other. We didn't know anyone there and it was too late to start socializing now. Some third-rate punk band started up in the back room but we didn't care enough to go have a look.

We left and went home pausing only to get some greasy food to quiet down my grog munchies. The next day we drove out of Adelaide and immediately felt better. The open highway was like a reviving tonic to us both. The feeling of going somewhere, being free, being unattached felt good and I think on some level we both understood that drifting was our natural state. That's why the highway felt so liberating, we were re-entering our natural element. Not for us the stability of the suburbs, give us a highway and a car with all our worldly possessions in the back.

We stopped at Kimba for lunch and Helen got me to take a photo of her with the Big Galah. We made it to Ceduna that night and stayed in the first motel we saw as we came into town. Seeing the tacky décor of the motel room and little soaps wrapped in plastic was like being home to us.

The next day we headed west along the Eyre Highway. We crossed the dog fence near Yalata and cheered being in the outback again. We stopped for lunch at Border Village and Helen got me to take a photo of her standing in two states at the border. I wonder how many thousands of tourists take that same photo every year. It just never gets old.

We arrived at Mundrabilla and settled in quickly. Because we were a couple we had the best and biggest room in the staff quarters, the rest of the staff were mostly transient backpackers only there for a few months at a time. The boss was a salty old veteran of the highway whom we'd already met when we worked at Madura.

The chef was a screaming queen named Justin who was gayer than Elton John and Oscar Wilde combined. I have never met anyone quiet like him. He was an outstanding chef who'd learned his trade in the finest kitchens in Sydney. He knew all the big names and had cooked for them all, his food was first rate and I asked him one day why he was working at a little roadhouse in the middle of nowhere.

'Isn't it obvious darling? Because I don't like the drugs but the drugs like me as dear old Marilyn said.'

It took me a whole day to realise he was quoting Marilyn Manson not Monroe. So I'm not a cultured person, shoot me.

As we spent more time there we realised the truth of what he said. Justin was a mess of substance abuse issues. He would drink until he was unconscious and he always followed the classic jollicose, bellicose, lachrymose, comatose pattern. Every now and then one of the truckies would sell him some powders. He preferred cocaine but would do speed if he couldn't get it, and he would go sideways in a major way.

One time he got his hands on some 'proper Sydney coke' from a passing truckie and stayed up all night cooking one Pavlova after another. Morning found him curled up on the floor, the kitchen destroyed and twenty-seven Pavlovas ready to eat. The boss was furious.

'What the fuck am I supposed to do with twenty-seven Pavlovas? How the fuck do you get that high and that stupid Justin? Now we have no eggs left, what the fuck am I supposed to use for people's breakfasts?'

We ended up eating all the Pavlovas and they were truly magnificent. You could have sold them for top dollar in any city bakery and not been ashamed. The man had issues but he more than made up for it with talent.

Over time I got more and more of Justin's backstory out of him. He had been born into wealth and privilege in Sydney. Sent to one of those posh schools that future Liberal Prime Ministers go to, he had started his downward spiral in his teenage years with a string of sexual indiscretions and drug misdemeanours that his family covered up as best they could.

He told me about some of his school escapades but I can't repeat them here since the boys involved have since grown up and become cabinet ministers in the current Liberal government. I have no money for lawyers if I get sued.

He flunked out and didn't get into university but salvaged some pride by getting an apprenticeship as a chef at a very prestigious Sydney restaurant. He did very well and big things were predicted for his future until his love of cocaine, MDMA and athletic young men interfered. What followed was a long string of disgraces. He had the distinction of being sacked from every fashionable restaurant in Sydney, no less than three cruise lines and several international hotel chains. Now he was working at a roadhouse in the middle of the Nullarbor.

His food was amazing and every truckie on the highway ate at our roadhouse. It was this boom in trade that made Justin unsackable, and the boss saw no sense in killing the goose that lays the golden egg even if that goose is a coke addicted queen with a drinking problem. The truckies were normally very redneck on the whole gay issue, but Justin earned their affection and even respect by giving quality banter along with his quality food. I remember seeing the place full of truckies eating dinner and Justin walked out of the kitchen higher than Hitler's gas bill to ask them at the top of his voice if they liked his special sauce. Laughs were had and Justin was deemed alright.

Justin decided he liked Helen and I straight away. He declared we were the most adorable couple and demanded that we breed immediately for we would surely produce the most beautiful children ever seen. He was of course drunk and high when he said this.

The social dynamic of the roadhouse became fixed around Justin, Helen and myself with the boss overseeing things and a stream of random backpackers making up the numbers. When you're in the outback time goes past like a dream. It's easy to see why some people end up spending their whole lives out here when almost by accident, one-week blends into another without a single care and before you know it you've spent a year in the middle of nowhere.

We had been in touch with Louise the whole time and she occasionally came and visited us at the roadhouse. Her transformation into bush matriarch was almost complete; someone meeting her for the first time would have no idea that she was the same person as the slightly druggie city girl I met at my cousin's share house.

About a year into our stay at Mundrabilla she had another baby and came to show us her new offspring. Helen was furious with jealousy but hid it so well that only I noticed. She made all the right clucky noises at the baby and all the right small talk with Louise.

Once Louise had left to go back to the station Helen had what can only be described as an epic rage tantrum. Being her significant other I copped the brunt of it before wisely retreating. I found her several hours later, calmer and very drunk sitting with Justin at the back of the staff quarters. She was slouched in a chair like she'd fallen asleep and had a big red wine stain on the front of her shirt. Justin was in a dressing gown and had a pint glass full of Shiraz in his hand.

'There you are, she's had her cry and feels better so you can breathe easier now, thank me later for my drama queen management skills. Helen darling, your lovely man is here to take you home.'

He shook her shoulder and Helen gave an incoherent grunt in response. I settled myself into the chair next to her and when she realised who I was she flopped her head into my lap and started crying.

'Classless, not a shred of decorum darling, did your mother teach you nothing?' Justin gently mocked while I tenderly stroked her hair and listened to her weep. Once I was pretty confident she had passed out I ventured to Justin that I thought it was a major overreaction on Helen's part. Louise had another baby and showed it to us, what was the big deal? Justin raised his eyebrow and looked at me like I was a total idiot.

'How is it you're a heterosexual man in his thirties and you don't know a thing about women? Actually scratch that, I think I just answered my own question, you are in for a miserable life, my boy.' He dismissed me with a wave of his hand and flounced off to his own room to continue drinking the day away. I was left with Helen asleep in my lap and reeking of red wine.

Eventually I carried her to our room and laid her down on our bed. She stirred but didn't fully wake as I lay down next to her and put my arm around her. I must have dozed off myself because I woke a few hours later when Helen raced to the toilet to vomit up the copious amounts of cheap and nasty Shiraz she'd consumed.

Something inside Helen was deeply hurt and I noticed she seemed sadder and more subdued, like a soldier who realises his cause is lost and his friends died for nothing but life still has to go on. She would latch onto me sometimes in the night when she thought I was asleep and silently cry into my shoulder or chest. I didn't know what to do or say and felt useless.

The thought occurred to me that a change of scenery would do us a world of good, but I needed to plan it so we didn't end up poor like we did in Adelaide. I had a friend in Perth who I used to work hospital security with and he had recently applied for and got a job with Correctional Services in WA working at the main prison in Perth. He told me it was a pretty sweet gig, good salary, loads of perks and since being tough on crime was always an election winner it was a guaranteed job for life so long as you didn't fuck it up.

I thought about it and a plan developed in my mind. We could move to Perth, I could work hospital security again and apply for the Corrections job when they next did a recruitment drive, my friend would go reference for me so the odds of me getting in were pretty good. It seemed feasible to me and when I suggested it to Helen she agreed to take the chance with me.

We gave notice and got organised. The boss was sad to see us go and told us all we had to do was ring and he'd take us back. Justin got weepy drunk and told us he would miss us. Louise came around to say goodbye and informed us she was pregnant again. Helen smiled politely but I could tell she was outraged.

The move to Perth was easy enough and we settled into life in the suburbs without too much drama. I got the security job in the hospital and started getting ready to apply for the prison job while Helen got a job at one of the big chain bottleshops at a nearby shopping centre.

We made a commitment that we weren't going to live like we had in Adelaide and started trying to be a little bit socially active. It didn't work out very well. Our jobs made our social life limited and the city people we did meet were a bit boring. Perhaps being in the middle of nowhere for so long had taken away our ability to socialize like normal people. We just couldn't make it work.

Without noticing it we drifted back to our pattern of keeping company with each other and not bothering too much with the outside world. On our days off we would take the train down to Fremantle and idle our time away pleasantly but we never really got too involved with the life of the city.

About six months into our time in Perth I got an email informing me that WA Corrections was recruiting again. I had everything ready to go and I applied with Helen's blessing. It was a long drawn out process as these things tend to be but I seemed to do well on the interviews and tests and I was cautiously optimistic.

A few months after I applied I got an email saying I was unsuccessful but I could apply again in six months if I wanted to. I was more upset about it than I let on to Helen and we both pondered what we were going to do. It took about a week before we both decided to get the hell out of the city and go back on the Nullarbor. I made the call to our old boss and he was ecstatic.

'About fucking time! I've had nothing but Muppets working here since you left. How soon can you get here? Can you pick up Justin and bring him back with you? He's in this rehab place down in Rockingham.'

It turned out that Justin had checked himself into a rehab clinic after a nasty health scare. According to the boss he was doing alright although I had my doubts, some people just aren't suited to a clean and sober lifestyle and in my opinion Justin was one of those people.

We arranged to go see him on a family visiting day that the rehab conducted every Sunday. Apparently we were the first and only people to visit Justin while he was there. The boss called every second week to find out when he was coming back to work but that hardly counts as family visiting. I almost didn't recognise Justin when we entered the grotty light green painted room that served as the rehab's family visiting centre. He had put on a little weight and the crazed look in his eyes was gone, in its place was a kind of sad puppy desperation that gave away how lost he really was.

It is a falsehood that everyone who has a drug and/or alcohol problem needs to get clean and sober. In most cases they will benefit from it but a significant percentage of addicts aren't capable of handling life without some form of chemical altering their reality. To deny them this security blanket is crueller than letting them go to their inevitable end under the comforting influence of the drugs which have made life bearable for them. Most people find this idea hard to accept but I've seen it firsthand many times, for many people life sober is unbearable and to inflict it on them because you think they need to live that way is nothing short of torture. Of course, do-gooders won't admit this and continue to interfere in other people's lives with generally disastrous results.

Justin was one such case; pure unmitigated reality was too much to bear for him, it would have been kinder to shoot him than let him experience life without drugs and alcohol. I could see in his eyes what a miserable time he'd been having in rehab, and I knew without doubt he was counting down the days until the programme finished and he could get off his face again.

We sat down and talked awkwardly with him about trifling things. He seemed so different from the Justin we knew and loved, it was honestly tragic to see such an effervescent person brought so low by unwanted sobriety. The rehab do-gooders would never understand what a horrible thing they had done to our friend, this funny, lovely, charming man who had never hurt anyone and only wanted to be off his face and having a good time until his body couldn't cope with the abuse anymore and gave up.

Justin told us he had a month left to go with the rehab programme and was keen to head back out to Mundrabilla the day he got out. We told him we were sick of the city as well and would gladly take him with us in a month's time. We made some more small talk and then left.

As Helen and I were driving back to our rented shitbox in the suburbs she started weeping as she sat beside me. I was alarmed at first and asked if she was alright and did she want me to pull over for a minute? She shook her head without saying anything. I realized her sadness wasn't something that I could do anything about, it was there, it would be there for the foreseeable future and that's all there was to it. I loved her but I knew there were limits on what I could do for her.

We got home and Helen lay down on the couch, still sad and barely coping. I felt I had to do something and a thought popped into my head which I decided to act on. I knelt down in front of her and held her hand while I spoke to her.

'So, we're going to head back out to the Nullarbor with Justin in a month, aren't we?' I said, and she nodded passively, her eyes still red and weepy.

'Let's get married the day Justin gets out, we could do it at the town hall or somewhere like that, Justin can be our witness, why not?'

She narrowed her eyes as if trying to determine that I was playing some cruel joke on her but satisfied that I wasn't, she agreed and kissed me gently while more tears formed in her eyes.

We started planning. Justin was keen to be our witness and said he would make an excellent bridesmaid. We discovered that under state law we needed two witnesses so Helen rang her father and he agreed to come down and attend.

Helen had told me a little about her dad. He had been a cop in Queensland, a detective in fact, before the Royal Commission into police corruption had named him and nearly sent him to jail. It seems he and some other detectives had their fingers in some very dirty pies and the only reason Helen's father hadn't ended up in prison for the rest of his life was because the key witnesses against him had ended up on the missing persons list.

After the fuss of the Royal Commission and his being sacked in disgrace from the force he'd moved to Darwin where he had recovered from his divorce by getting himself a Thai wife half his age. Helen grew up blaming her mother for the breakup of their family and loving her dad despite his being in another state. She visited him as often as she could and the half brothers and sisters he'd fathered with the Thai wife she treated as her real family, while she cut her mother off almost completely.

I was happy to meet him and happy that Helen was happy. Life was actually looking up. The day came to pick up Justin from rehab and we waited patiently in the foyer while the do-gooder in chief tried to give him one final lecture about attending meetings, working the program and all that bollocks.

I say 'tried to' because Justin was having none of it and went full angry queen mode telling them all to fuck off. He loudly informed them that he would be drunk within half an hour of leaving this godforsaken modern concentration camp and he had never intended to remain sober but had just been using the place as a rest stop between binges while his health recovered.

Justin had intended this declaration to be shocking. I think he had probably practiced his speech in the mirror. The do-gooders had heard it all before. They looked at him like a parent would look at a child throwing a tantrum. The only difference was they couldn't just spank him.

We had come prepared and had a six pack of bourbon and coke cans in the car. Justin saw them and screamed 'thank the lord it's bogan juice!' before inhaling them at a remarkable rate. As we drove to the city Justin got drunker and more like his normal self.

We had already given up our flat and booked ourselves in at a nice hotel in the city. Justin got a room at a cheaper and sleazier hotel down the street. We were booked to get married by the registrar at one that afternoon so we told Justin to be there and be at least functional enough to sign his name to the official paperwork. He promised he would but I had my doubts.

Helen and I got dressed up in the nicest clothes we owned and headed down to meet her dad. Just before we left the hotel I asked her if she still wanted to go through with it. We could always do a runner if she wanted, it wouldn't put anyone else out that much. She wouldn't hear of it. I was very pleased.

We met Helen's dad at the town hall and he shook my hand and told me to call him John. He seemed a good bloke and I immediately took a liking to him. He introduced his Thai wife who I noticed was only a year or two older than Helen and proudly showed us his kids. The kids loved Helen like a big sister and were super excited by the whole shebang, the oldest girl hung onto Helen's hand and fussed over her dress and flowers.

We were standing around like this in the foyer of the Perth Town Hall when Justin made his entrance. He was wearing a frilly bridesmaid dress he had acquired from who knows where and was drunk as a lord.

'Darlings I'm here! I'm no virgin it's true but white really suits me, don't you think?'

Helen and I laughed and waved him over while John and his wife looked a little worried by this turn of events. The youngest of Helen's half-siblings looked at Justin and said the first childishly innocent thing that popped into his head.

'You're a boy but you're wearing a dress like a girl,' he said in that way of stating the obvious that children often have.

'And you're a half-caste pretending to be Australian but I'll be nice to you if you'll be nice to me, darling.' Justin's cutting, bitchy sarcasm always came out best when he was drunk but I froze for a moment anticipating how John would react. I thought we were going to have a punch up at our wedding; how delightfully Bogan that would be.

John laughed and slapped Justin on the back. Apparently he appreciated a spot of quality banter and had no great sensitivities concerning his children's race. I had a feeling they were going to become great drinking buddies and as things turned out I was right.

We walked in and got on with it. Helen and I said our vows in front of the registrar, Justin and John signed the paperwork as witnesses and we were married. We all went off to our hotel for drinks.

John and Justin started a truly epic bender and got on like a house on fire. It was an odd sight, the queen in a bridesmaid's dress and the middle-aged disgraced ex-Queensland cop getting rip-roaringly drunk together and telling funny stories. They seemed to find some common bond. My theory is that they both knew they had blown their lives in pretty major ways, John with his corruption and Justin with drugs, and this made them brothers of a sort. The fellowship of men who've wandered off the path.

Helen and I kept her siblings and their mother company. They were good kids and I liked them straight away, the Thai wife was a fairly quiet person but fundamentally a good soul. They seemed to be doing okay as a family and that's plenty.

After a while they went back to their hotel leaving the two men at the bar and Helen and me alone.

'Should we join those two?' I asked her, pointing in the direction of the mess that was Justin in his now soiled bridesmaid's dress.

'No, leave them be, they seem to get on alright. Let's go upstairs and call it a day.'

We got up and told them we were packing it in for the day. We told Justin to be functional tomorrow because we had to start the drive out to Mundrabilla. Helen hugged her dad and thanked him for coming all the way from Darwin.

We got to our very expensive room and made love, I nodded off straight after and didn't wake for several hours. When I got up Helen was sitting by the window wrapped in a towel staring out at the Perth skyline. I wrapped a towel around myself and joined her by the window.

'Hey sleepy head, thought you were out for the count,' she said.

'Nah I'm good, just a big day; how you feeling?'

'Good, just watching the lights in the city; you want something to eat? I was going to order some room service.'

'Yeah in a bit, no rush; penny for your thoughts?'

She leant her head into my chest and I held her a bit tighter. She was silent for a few moments and I thought she was going to stay that way until she spoke quietly, timidly, as if frightened to disturb the peaceful scene outside the window.

'We haven't amounted to much, have we? All these years of drifting around and we're not much better off than when we started. I used to get really upset by that. I got bitterly jealous of Louise because of the life she'd made for herself but now I'm sort of okay with it. We are what we are, the smart thing to do is make the best of it. We'll go back out to the Nullarbor, we'll save some money and then in a year or so we'll move to Darwin. My dad can help us get started up there. We'll make a life for ourselves and settle down. We won't achieve anything massive or set the world on fire but we'll do okay. Years from now we'll remember how we started and we'll be happy with where we are.'

I held her close and was happy.

The next day we got up early, paid the hotel bill and went to pick up Justin. He was waiting on the sidewalk just outside his hotel, apparently they'd kicked him out because he'd brought back some random guys he met somewhere and spent all night doing coke and fucking very loudly.

He flaked into the back seat; everything he owned in the world was with everything we owned in the world all piled together in the boot. We drove east onto the highway that would take us out of the city and back to the Nullarbor. The early morning rush had started and there were a lot of cars heading the opposite way from us, commuters doing their daily grind into the city and their jobs which they probably hated.

The suburbs started to thin out into bush and farmland. Helen put on a Smiths CD and the strains of 'Hand in Glove' filled the car. I smiled at her, she smiled back and held my hand, we started singing along, gently at first but getting louder and more dramatic as we hammed it up doing air guitar and bad Morrissey impressions. We laughed, we were happy.

'Fuck's sake you two, if I'd known you were going to be so sickeningly sweet I'd have never agreed to be your bridesmaid. Have a fucking baby, move to the suburbs and be done with it already,' Justin ranted before laying down to nurse his hangover.

We headed further into the bush and our future such as it was.

A ROW OF BOTTLEBRUSH TREES

They let me sit out in the garden most afternoons. Once the medication rounds have been done there is no good reason to keep me cooped up inside. I sit out here for as long as they let me. It won't be long before I'm too sick to do this so it's best to enjoy it while I can.

I sit out here and enjoy the sunshine. There is a row of bottlebrush trees forming a rough hedge around the garden. This time of year they are flowering. Tufts of crimson blossom stand out like explosions against the green leaves. Birds come and feed, Rosellas, Honeyeaters and Port Lincoln Parrots, adding more colour to the display. Nature showing off her vitality to us poor bastards dying in this grim old hospital.

I remember when I was a kid. The little beach town I grew up in had bottlebrushes planted around the place too. They used to grow between the street and the front of people's houses. Every spring they'd flower and give the whole town a crimson glow.

I don't recall paying them much attention when I was a kid. Young people don't tend to notice things like that as much as old people. I remember we used to race past those trees, down those sleepy streets, in a hurry to get to the beach. Always in a hurry to get into the water. Heedless of the sun and the heat. Full of life and energy in a town that was permanently asleep in the long Australian summer.

There were bottlebrush trees in the house I lived in when I first moved to the city now that I think about it. It was a share house, a bunch of us in our early twenties were living there, doing Uni or working the shitty jobs you get when you're young and clueless. It was an old house, the owner didn't maintain it very well, I think he was just sitting on it waiting for the prices in the area to go up. In the meantime he rented it out to us rabble. I wonder if it's still there? Or has it been knocked down by some developer and turned into units for Chinese students?

There was a row of bottlebrush trees out front, formed up along the fence in a raggedy line. I remember spewing up in them once. I'd come home so drunk I could barely stand let alone walk and the kebab I'd had an hour before decided to repeat on me. The things you do when you're young and silly.

I remember when I was 28, Sarah and I had shacked up together in a little flat. There were bottlebrush trees in the little garden out the front, pretty small things that barely flowered. Some guy used to come from the real estate agent to water them every week. The block of flats was basic and dull. Full of young working people trying to get ahead in life. The rent was cheap because the suburb wasn't that great.

Sarah and I had plans, we were going to save money and get ahead, maybe put down a deposit for our own place. We were in love and full of hope for the future. Then she took the test.

She was late but hadn't thought too much about it, she'd often been a little late, then she was a lot late. She got a pregnancy test from the supermarket and put it on the kitchen bench where it stayed for several days while she worried a little more. Finally, she did it. I sat in the lounge room of our little flat while she peed on the stick. A sudden shout 'CHRIS!' and I raced to the toilet where she was sitting, pants around her ankles, staring at the stick. With a trembling hand she turned it, so I could see the result.

Sarah spoke in a quiet, terrified voice 'I'm pregnant' telling me what I already knew. I walked outside, numb with shock, trying to process what was happening. I remember staring at those little bottlebrushes and listening to the traffic in the neighbourhood while I thought about what we were going to do.

I remember the primary school our daughter went to. Nice enough place, the teachers actually cared and tried hard and I think that made a lot of difference. It had some bottlebrush trees around the oval too. I remember going for some school sports thing Hannah was in. All us parents standing on the edge of the oval watching the kids run around, applauding their efforts and chatting amongst ourselves.

I remember when it was all done walking hand in hand with Hannah across the oval on our way back to the car. Her little voice asking me if I'd seen her run, just a little girl needing her father's approval. We walked past those bottlebrushes if I remember right. The crimson flowers lighting up the day as we walked, content in our family happiness.

I don't know how much longer I'll be allowed to sit out here and enjoy this garden with its row of bottlebrush trees. They used words like 'aggressive' and 'inoperable' to describe my cancer. When I asked for specifics and times they were less confident. Maybe six months, maybe four, they couldn't say with any certainty. They were sure that I would never leave the hospital alive. That much is clear. So I sit and wait and watch this garden with its bottlebrushes and birds. Enjoying the sunshine while I can.

THE FAILURE

If you are my age and you were a teenager in the nineties in Australia then you remember alternative rock. It was the boom time for that genre. Triple J were constantly playing great guitar bands from right here in Australia as well as imported stuff. You're probably mentally rattling off the names right now, You Am I, Grinspoon, Jebediah, Regurgitator, Magic Dirt, The Superjesus and so on and so on.

You probably listened to Triple J and went to festivals in summer like most of us did, had your favourite bands and played the CDs in your shitbox first car with the P plates on it. It was a good time or at least it seems so in my memory. If it wasn't the best of times it certainly had one of the best soundtracks of any time.

In the nineties I was young and alive and it seemed like I could do anything with my life. Now I'm in my thirties and the whole thing seems a grim struggle to avoid the poorhouse and that's on a good day. When I listen to those bands from that time I can capture a little of that spark of youth and life again. It's a good feeling.

What happened to those bands and the people in them? Life happened to them the same as it happens to everyone else. Some of them broke up but the individuals still make music in one form or another. Some became drug casualties like so many musicians before and since. Some bands have reformed and are working the nostalgia circuit or even in a few cases putting out new material that is worth a listen.

I met Adam in 2013 when I was working at Nullarbor roadhouse in South Australia. I didn't realise who he was for nearly a week. He just seemed like another poverty-stricken bloke so desperate for a job that he'd come out to the middle of nowhere. We get them all the time, when you've come to a dead end in life the Nullarbor will still take you, plenty of room for lost souls out here so long as they can stand behind a counter and serve fuel to idiot tourists for seven hours a day.

His body language gave the impression that life had beaten him down till he was beyond resisting in any meaningful sense. When I listened to him talk this impression grew stronger. He wore clothes that had been fashionable once but were obviously getting old. His hair was still long in that classic nineties style but a bald patch was starting to appear right on the crown of his head, making him look more tragic old has been than grunge guitar hero.

In the first week or so of his being at the roadhouse I kept thinking I knew him from somewhere. I'd worked in pubs around Adelaide for years so I was always bumping into people from that scene but I couldn't quite place this guy. Eventually I asked him where I knew him from. He looked at me like he was assessing my age for a few minutes before replying.

'I was in a band called Waratah Farm back in the day. You're about the right age, you might remember us.'

I did and it all came back to me instantly. They'd had an album out in 1996 that had three big singles which were flogged to death on Triple J all that year. I'd had it on cassette and used to play it a lot in my first car, a rusted out old Magna with P plates on the back and cigarette burns on the floor of the passenger side.

I remembered they put out a second album in late 1997 which wasn't quite as good but still listenable and then a third one in 1999 which was almost totally ignored. I went to see them in early 1997, my first big gig in the city, they were touring with You Am I and Powderfinger and it was one of the best gigs I can remember.

As the memories raced through my mind I looked at the frankly rather pathetic middle-aged man beside me who was desperate enough to come out to the Nullarbor for a job and I couldn't help but ask, what the fuck happened?

He wasn't defensive about it and calmly told me his tale of woe with an air of resignation and defeat.

'After the third album went nowhere in '99 the record company dropped us. The whole alternative guitar rock thing was going out of fashion anyway so we weren't the only band dumped. We did the sums and realised we hadn't made that much money. We were big in Australia for about three or four years, it's not like we were the Rolling Stones or anything, a band that's only big in Australia for a few years doesn't get rich. I got depressed for a little while but pulled out of it and tried to get another band going. Seemed a reasonable thing to do, dust yourself off and get back in the saddle and all that. The band I started went nowhere, maybe half a dozen gigs, no interest from the public, nothing. People just didn't care anymore.'

'I tried doing some solo acoustic stuff. I wrote a bunch of fairly good songs, very folksy and melodic, tried them out at some small venues. No one cared. There were plenty of other people doing that sort of thing and most of them did it better than me. I was starting to realise that maybe I'd had my one and only shot at the big time.'

'I got even more depressed. It really hit me that the high point of my life was in the past. The best days I was ever going to have had been and gone. I turned thirty in 2002 and felt like killing myself for a whole year. What was I supposed to do with my life? I'd put my heart and soul into my band and my music. I'd practiced every day since I was ten, my entire life had been dedicated to the goal of being in a band and making music. I'd had my day in the sun and now it was over. Statistically I could probably expect to live until I was seventy or eighty; what was I supposed to do with all that time? Everything I'd worked for and cared about had been and gone. Was I supposed to just sit around twiddling my thumbs until I died of old age?'

He paused and drew breath, the enormity of a life with no real purpose stretching out before him. I was hooked on his every word. There was something about his story that really resonated with me. Perhaps I saw my own life mirrored a little more dramatically in his. For both of us the good times were done and gone. Only the grim business of survival remained.

'I got even more depressed, I drank too much, I tried suicide but woke up in hospital cursing the person who found me. They put me in the psych ward for a while and I did the whole medication, therapy and hospital routine for a couple of years. I didn't get any better but all the useless social workers and psych doctors got to poke and prod me and write reports about my mental health.'

'For a few years there I was one of those sad losers you see hanging around clinics and psych wards. Shuffling from all the medication I was on, totally aimless, nowhere to be and nothing to do, I spent years on pills numbed out and watching daytime TV. Eventually some little scrap of the will to live managed to get through the medication haze and I knew I had to get off the pills and out of the psych system or I would be stuck in it my whole life.'

'I did a runner to Darwin. I'd heard that the authorities couldn't get you up there. I don't know if that's true or not. Turns out the hospital people didn't give a fuck that I wasn't going to the clinic and taking my meds anymore. I was just a file in a computer to them. A number for them to justify their funding from the government. If I lived or died or fucked off to the NT didn't really matter. No one came looking for me. I lived like a dog for the first few weeks. I effectively detoxed from the meds while I was on the bus to Darwin. It was hell.'

'I was on a disability pension so I had a little bit of money to keep from starving. I got a room at some boarding house up there that was full of old alcoholics who'd come to Darwin to drink themselves to death. It stank; you ever smelt that sweat that comes from old guys who've been drinking goon all day? The whole building smelt like that. I lived on tinned spaghetti and toast. It felt good to have a clear head again after those years on meds. I used to walk around Darwin during the day. Not doing anything, just walking and thinking, I still had no idea what I was going to do. I was getting older and I had nothing to show for my life except a couple of hits back in the nineties that were only ever played for nostalgia value now.'

'After a couple of years in Darwin I decided to get a job and try to live like a normal person. My resumé was pathetic. Imagine it, guitarist and singer in a band that was moderately successful between 1996 and 1999 then dropkick with mental health problems since then. Who the fuck was going to hire me? One of the old alcos at the boarding house told me about the roadhouses in the bush, how they couldn't get people and would hire almost anyone who showed up, how you lived on site and got housed and fed by the boss so you could drink or save your entire pay every week if you wanted.'

'I didn't have any better ideas so that's what I did and here I am.'

Here he was indeed. I took a few moments to try and digest what he'd told me. It was one of the best tales of woe I've ever heard and I've heard plenty in my time out bush so I consider myself an expert on tales of woe. There are always people coming out here who've done their dash and made a mess of their lives. That's the thing about the Nullarbor; when you've made a dog's breakfast of your life the highway will still take you.

I struggled to think of something empathic to say but he didn't seem inclined to hear it. He shrugged his shoulders as if to say 'such is life' and walked off to the staff kitchen to get himself some lunch. I stood for a while on that spot out the back of the roadhouse watching the crows fly across the big empty nothing that surrounded us. It occurred to me that this had to be a massive come down from the life he'd once had.

There was nothing I could do for him. His problems ran deep and were probably beyond any human help. I decided the best thing I could do was just be cool about it and treat him like a decent human being.

I stayed at Nullarbor roadhouse for another six months. Adam got the hang of the job and seemed to fit into the routine of life out there. He never lost that beaten down, defeated look though. When I left for greener pastures I told him to take care and if he wanted to stay in touch I'd be happy to. He was very non-committal about it and I didn't press the issue.

About two years later I passed through there again and stayed the night. I hadn't really set the world on fire but I'd managed to do alright in my new life in Perth. I felt like I'd managed to escape the rut I'd been in when I went out to the Nullarbor and now that I was feeling comfortable and almost middle class I was nostalgic for the old days. I kept thinking about Adam and all the other misfits I'd known out there back in the day. I got excited to see if any of them were still around.

As is usually the case there was almost no staff remaining from my time. Two years is a long time on the Nullarbor. I spoke to the manager and explained that I used to work there and asked if Adam was still around.

'Don't know any Adam. We've been here four months, he must have left before then. Was he a mate of yours?'

'Yeah,' I replied, 'he was a good bloke. It's a pity I lost contact.'

'Life goes like that sometimes; people drift and you lose them, nothing to be done about it,' he said, and grabbed me another beer from the fridge.

A PISTOL AND A FRENCH GIRL

It was my own fault I got bit by a Huntsman. Anyone who has spent time in the bush knows that you never put your hands or your feet anywhere your eyes haven't checked out first. I knew this but forgot it that day until the bite of a freakishly large Huntsman reminded me.

I was fiddling around with some of the wrecks out the back of the roadhouse. Every roadhouse on the Nullarbor has a pile of wrecks somewhere out the back. They are the ones that didn't make it, shitbox vans that backpackers bought on eBay for $800 and thought they could drive from Perth to Byron Bay, people who tried to drive after dark and discovered too late that by the time you see the kangaroo on the road there isn't much you can do about it and whatever else has drifted through and not quite made it.

I was looking for a part for an old Falcon I was trying to fix. We had plenty of wrecked Falcons out the back so I thought my luck might hold and I might be able to find the part I needed instead of coughing up cash for it in Kalgoorlie. I opened the bonnet of one old station wagon and that's when it happened. I felt the bite like two needles in my hand and saw the spider a few seconds too late to do anything about it.

The pain began immediately; if you've never been bitten by a Huntsman I can only describe the pain as a chemical burn. As though someone had put industrial strength bleach into an open wound.

To my credit I didn't panic. I was savvy enough to know my bush creepy crawlies and I knew a Huntsman when I saw one. I knew that Huntsman bites were usually not fatal but I also knew I was in for a time of it. I headed to the office straight away and told the manager I needed the flying doctor right now. The useless fat prick looked quite miffed that I'd interrupted his lunch but got with it quickly and rang the Royal Flying Doctor Service for me.

I was getting very sick now, breaking out in sweat and feeling like I wanted to throw up. I spoke to the doctor on the phone and he asked me questions about what I was feeling and if I could be sure of the identity of the spider. I held my rising panic and answered him calmly. He assured me the plane was on its way and I should prepare to meet them at the airstrip.

I hung up the phone and felt a sudden urge to spew. I raced out the back to where the bins were and let loose a torrent of vomit. Adding insult to injury I was sweating more than I ever have before or since. My shirt and hair looked like I'd been under the sprinkler for most of the day and I struggled to keep my eyes clear.

I shuffled back to the staff quarters in a lot of pain and began organising a bag to take with me. I got a change of clothes and my shaving stuff and sat in the office to wait. The maintenance guy was there and he drove me to the airstrip at the top of the hill. We waited in his ute, every twenty minutes or so I had to open the door to spew on the red dust outside and the chemical burn feeling was only growing stronger.

At length the plane arrived and the doctor examined me right there in the dust, heat and flies. He asked me questions and looked at the bite. You could see twin fang marks all black and swollen on my hand and when I vomited on his shoes he decided it was time to get me on the plane.

We lifted off and once the plane levelled out they stuck an IV drip in me. I think it had something in it because the rest of the flight is a blur. I remember spewing a couple more times, stopping for refuelling in Kalgoorlie and then a bumpy landing at Jandakot airport in Perth followed by an ambulance drive to Royal Perth Hospital.

I was wheeled into the hospital feeling truly woeful and the doctors got on my case fairly quickly. I can't complain about the medical attention I received but being a public hospital in the centre of the city the place was full of junkies in various states of disrepair making a racket. I made a mental note to cough up for private health insurance so that next time the flying doctor took me in I would go to a nicer hospital.

I spent two nights there and whatever anti-venom they gave me seemed to work. I stopped vomiting, the chemical burn sensation at the site of the wound ceased and I started to feel a lot better. When they were satisfied that I was past danger they started organising my discharge. The tricky thing now was getting back to the Nullarbor. The flying doctor is a wonderful service and I won't hear a bad word against them but they only take you one way. Some social worker type from the hospital spoke to me and I explained that if she could organise me a train ticket to Kalgoorlie and then a bus ticket to Norseman I could hitch a ride with one of our regular truckies from there.

This was fairly quickly arranged and I was discharged not long after that. The train didn't leave until the next day so I had to find a place to stay the night. I knew a cheap motel on Murray Street so I headed there and booked in. First order of business was to have a long hot shower and get the stink of hospital and sweat off me. It felt like the spider's venom had somehow seeped through my sweat glands and made my skin toxic and disgusting.

After that I began to think about what I was going to do with my unplanned day in the city. I thought about the train trip to Kalgoorlie tomorrow and realised I needed to get myself something to read. There was a groovy little science fiction bookshop hidden away in the city that I knew of so I headed there and got myself some old school Asimov for the trip. After that I went to Northbridge for Chinese and then spent a lazy evening watching TV in my motel room.

The next morning I was up at sparrow's fart to catch the train. I waited around on the platform at East Perth barely awake, sipping a nasty machine coffee while they put our luggage on board. They let us on and I sat down with my book ignoring the safety and welcome announcements over the train's PA. I'd been on this service plenty of times before and didn't need to hear this bollocks again.

I mostly read or snoozed for the duration of the trip, the countryside passed by in a blur and with the exception of our brief stop in Merredin I took no notice at all. We were in Kalgoorlie before I knew it. I had to stay a night in Kalgoorlie and catch the bus to Norseman the next day. I booked into a motel and while I was idling away the evening my boss from the roadhouse called me.

'When you get to Norseman meet up with this French girl at the BP there, she's coming out to work with us for a while. Get a ride with one of the regular truckies and look after her.'

'Since when were we hiring new people again?'

'That Kiwi chick we had behind the bar spat the dummy and quit. This French girl has been working at a pub in Esperance for a few months so she'll do. Look after her and don't be a sleaze and try to root her. At least wait until she gets to the roadhouse.'

He hung up and I had a think about which truckies would be coming through tomorrow. It was a Wednesday so I thought my best bet was Jackson; he drove a fridge truck back and forth from Adelaide to Perth for one of the major supermarket chains. He was regular as clockwork and not a dickhead so I decided I would aim to hitch a ride with him. The presence of this French girl shouldn't be a big deal.

The next day I caught the bus from Kalgoorlie to Norseman. It's a crap service and I don't like taking it if I can avoid it. It's usually half full of people who let their feral kids run up and down the aisle making a racket and a handful of backpackers who don't know any better. I tried to tune out the brats and finish my book as best I could and it wasn't that long before we arrived in Norseman.

I went to the big BP on the corner to wait for Jackson to arrive. My boss had texted me the French girl's number so after I got a coffee and sat down I gave her a call to see where she was. A French voice answered the phone so I thought I had best explain myself.

'Hi, I'm the bloke from Madura roadhouse, you're hitching a ride with me apparently.'

'Yes, where are you?'

'I'm in the big BP in Norseman having a coffee, where are you?'

'I'm over the other side, I think I can see you.'

I looked up and sure enough there she was across the half empty café. She hung up and walked over to where I was smiling as she introduced herself. Her name was Anna, she was doing the traditional backpacker thing, going around Australia, working in pubs and roadhouses to fund it all and having a great time.

We got chatting and I told her all about my recent misadventure with the Huntsman spider. I showed her what remained of the bite mark. She was lapping it up. I've come across this before, Europeans love all that 'Crocodile Hunter' type stuff, show them some snakes in the bush and they pretty much wet themselves with excitement. The female backpackers are especially excited by it and I've removed more than one pair of European panties simply by showing them a snake in the wild. The trick is to talk it up but try and sound casual about it, like you deal with lethal snakes and spiders every day and it's no big thing to you.

Anyway, we chatted while we waited for Jackson to arrive and soon enough I saw his truck bearing the corporate logo on its side pull in. I waited until he got out of the truck before walking over. He saw me and smiled, shouting greetings across the concrete forecourt of the servo.

'I hear you've been in the wars, took on a Huntsman and lost, got a free ride with the flying quack.'

'Yeah my own damn fault, didn't look where I was putting my hand, won't make that mistake again. This is Anna by the way, she's coming to work at the roadhouse with me, we're hoping to catch a ride with you if that's alright.'

'Yeah no worries mate, sling your shit in the cab and hop in, I won't be long. How you doing Anna? Watch out for this one, he's a dodgy character.'

We climbed into the truck and stashed our gear out of the way as best we could. Anna was excited, I don't think she'd ever been in a proper road train before. I could tell she was thinking about how she would tell her friends back home about her big outback adventure. She was getting to live the 'Jack Kerouac meets Crocodile Dundee' fantasy that so many of these Euro tourists have.

Jackson paid for his diesel, the truck pulled out onto the highway and headed east from Norseman through the endless dry woodlands and small hills that seem to go on forever until you hit Balladonia. Jackson and I talked shit about other truckies we knew, muppets working at the various roadhouses, just general highway gossip. Anna listened but didn't say much, she didn't know any of the people we were talking about so I don't suppose there was anything she could add to the conversation.

We passed Balladonia just as the light was failing and by the time we hit the ninety mile straight it was dark. In my own car I would never have dared drive this stretch after dark but trucks do it all the time.

We were halfway across the straight when it happened. It was as though the great God Murphy saw us making light of his law and decided to smite us for our presumption. Jackson had just finished saying that there didn't seem to be much wildlife out tonight when a camel appeared in the headlights and it was too late to dodge it.

The noise a truck makes when it hits a camel cannot be described, it has to be heard. I heard Jackson shout 'cunt!' and Anna screamed a little girly scream more appropriate to a five year old. Metal hit camel flesh and the truck moved no more. I quickly checked that everyone was alright, Anna was shaken but fine, I was okay but Jackson seemed to have broken his hand somehow. Best guess was he had it looped awkwardly in the steering wheel and the impact must have broken it. He wouldn't be driving anymore tonight, he was in quite a bit of pain.

We gingerly stepped out of the truck, Jackson nursing his busted hand, to check the damage and decide what to do. The camel was still alive, crippled but full of fight, spitting at us and roaring like a great wounded behemoth in the night. We couldn't even begin to try and sort out the truck until this camel was moved, it was beyond moving itself and it was spitting and biting at us every time we came close.

We retreated to a safe distance and pondered our situation. There might not be another truck to help us for hours, this camel wouldn't just die quietly and until it was dead and removed we couldn't do anything about our truck. Jackson was in a lot of pain by now, his hand was looking mangled and swelling rapidly, he spoke up and said he had a pistol behind the driver's seat of the truck. If I went and got it we could shoot the camel and maybe move it out of the way.

I wasted no time and got the pistol from its hiding place. There was no way this gun was legal and I could only imagine the dodgy characters Jackson had bought it from but that was irrelevant right now. Broken down in the dark, miles from anywhere, with an aggressive crippled camel that needed killing, I couldn't afford to ask questions.

It was a black 9mm Beretta. The serial number had been filed off so I assumed this had gone walkabout from somewhere. I remembered reading that this model weapon was the standard issue sidearm of US forces so it probably came from one of the Yank bases up in the NT. Some solider needing extra cash for drugs, gambling or the like had probably stolen it from the base and sold it to bikies. Happens all the time.

The camel was swinging its head wildly back and forth so there was no way I was going to be able to get an accurate shot from any sort of distance. I needed to immobilise its great big head somehow. Jackson came up with the idea of him and Anna distracting it while I came up behind and got its neck in between my legs to brace its head for the fatal shot. It seemed the best and only plan we had so we set to it.

Jackson led slowly, his hand was obviously in agony and he nursed it gingerly; Anna followed him. They shouted and made noises to get the animal's attention. It rewarded them with vicious and well-aimed spit. I weaselled my way around the back of the beast and when I felt the timing was right I tackled its neck from behind. I got it between my legs like Jackson had suggested but I didn't realise how muscular and strong a camel's neck is. It bucked and kicked against me and I felt a ridge of muscle and bone on the top of the neck make hard contact with my balls. I winced but held firm. The motion of its head was much reduced now and I felt confident I could get a good clean headshot. I shouted at Jackson and Anna to get out of the way in case the bullet ricocheted and took aim.

My shot was true. The bullet entered the beast's head from the rear and exited via the mouth, taking several of its teeth with it. A second or two after the teeth had hit the road a slow moving goop of brain matter and blood drizzled out of the gap where the teeth had been. I heard Anna gasp and Jackson mutter 'fuck me' and I realized I now had bits of camel skull and brains on my shoes.

Now we were left with the problem of getting the animal off the road. Jackson's hand was useless now but he could shove from one side with his shoulder while Anna and I got on the other side and pulled. This camel weighed at least a ton so we made negligible progress, after half an hour busting our arses we had moved it maybe half a foot. We paused for a breather and Jackson suggested we try moving the truck around it instead; he thought it might be possible if we did a 'seventeen fucken point turn' and for lack of better options we agreed.

Jackson couldn't handle the steering wheel with his hand busted like it was so I would drive while he sat next to me and gave me instructions, Anna would stand on the road and give us directions, letting us know how close or far we were to getting around the carcass. I got in the driver's seat and followed Jackson's instructions, I ground the gears fairly badly while

Anna guided us as best she could waving her hands around like a deck officer on an aircraft carrier. What Jackson had predicted being a seventeen point turn ended up closer to a thirty point turn but eventually we were clear of the carcass and able to move along.

Anna jumped in the truck next to Jackson who sat in the middle to guide my driving and we got underway, I had never driven a big truck like this before and I'm sure I did it badly although Jackson was starting to get weary from the pain so he didn't say much to me. I kept the truck at about eighty kms an hour so it was slow going but I had no idea if another camel was out there in the darkness.

Eventually we pulled into Caiguna and with a bit of a bump and hiss I parked the truck out the front of the roadhouse. We all piled out as Dazza the nightshift guy came out for a look.

'Fuck me, you've had a shocker by the looks of it, what happened?'

'Hit a camel, I'm in a bit of pain here, bloke,' Jackson said. 'I've broken my hand, can I use your phone to call the flying doctor?' Dazza directed him to the phone inside. Anna and I wandered inside, unsure what to do next. I thought that Jackson's hand was almost certainly broken so he would likely get flown out by the RFDS tomorrow morning at first light. Meanwhile we were still 150 kms from Madura with no plan for getting there.

We made ourselves coffees from the little truckie refreshment station inside the roadhouse and sat down to think about our next move. The TV was on in the corner and Dazza had tuned it in to SBS for the late night tits and ninjas film with subtitles. I half-heartedly watched some of it while I thought about what we were going to do. I decided I should call the roadhouse and let them know what had happened.

The useless fat prick answered the phone and I told him of our misadventure with the camel. He thought about it for a few minutes and said we should get rooms at Caiguna tonight and he'd send someone up in the morning.

'Get a feed as well and tell the Caiguna mob to bill us at Madura.'

I hung up and went and found Dazza and Jackson out the back. Dazza was dosing up Jackson with what little painkillers he could find in the roadhouse first aid kit. The flying doctor couldn't get here till morning so Jackson was in for a miserable night. I told Dazza what my boss had said and he was cool, he told me to grab keys from the hooks above the counter and write down what rooms we were in, he'd deal with it later.

I went back out front and explained the situation to Anna, she nodded and I grabbed us the keys to two rooms next door to each other. We dumped our stuff and went back to the roadhouse for a feed. Dazza made us both burgers with bacon, cheese and eggs, a truckie heart attack special. Anna found it hard to get through a whole one. We watched the tits and ninjas movie on TV and tried to relax after all the drama we'd had on the highway.

Dazza was full-on playing nurse to Jackson now. He'd strapped up his hand, dosed him with painkillers and was fussing over him like an old woman. I knew from personal experience that the night shift gig at a roadhouse like this is boring as batshit so truth be told he was probably grateful for the excitement.

Anna and I said goodnight to them and headed back to our rooms. When I got to the door of my room I went to turn and say goodnight to her when I realised she was right next to me, next thing I knew she had grabbed me and forced her tongue down my throat. She ended up staying in my room that night and when the maintenance guy from Madura came to pick us up in the morning she had to do a quick walk of shame next door to get her stuff.

We made it back to Madura and life went on, Anna started work and seemed to enjoy it, my adventure with the Huntsman became a good yarn to tell to travellers and a few months later I accidently got Anna pregnant but that's another story for another time.

A LITTLE FLAT IN DOVER COURT

Sit down mate, you're making the place look untidy! Here, have a cuppa and sit out on the balcony with me. It's only small and we're not quite high enough to see the ocean but I like to sit out here and have my cup of coffee. I like watching the trains go past. Yeah, the good old Fremantle line, Victoria Street is the closest station here, just up the street and past the servo. I listen to the trains at night when I'm lying in bed. I find it soothing.

How long have I been here? Well it's getting on towards twenty years. I was nineteen years old when I got this flat, rent was a lot cheaper then too, I got this flat the same week as I got my job down at the bottleshop. Still at the bottle-o and still in this flat. Some people might think it's odd to stay in the one place and the one job for so long, but I say if you're happy, why leave?

I remember those early years here, I lived a quiet life then too, I suppose I've always been a quiet sort, wild parties and socializing just aren't my thing. I worked at the bottleshop most days and chilled out at home with a book or some music on my days off. Yeah, see that spare bedroom? I turned it into my books and music room, all my CDs and records in there, bookshelves full of old books that I've read over the years.

Might be worth money to a collector but I doubt it. Couldn't bear to be parted from it all anyway so it's a moot point really.

I used to go to gigs back then. Perth had a lot of cool indie bands and whatnot, so I used to catch the train into the city to go see them. I loved all that scene. I tried to make friends and get a band started but I was too shy to talk to people at the gigs. I put up a sign at a record store in the city to get a band started but nobody rang.

So, I mostly stuck to the quiet pleasures, the cinema, my ever-expanding record collection and good books, to help pass the time. Life has always been pleasant enough. You just have to learn to enjoy the simple things, that's the trick, I think. Every Sunday morning, I have a big fry-up breakfast; bacon, mushrooms, beans and eggs on toast. Nothing like it. Then I usually settle in with a good book or I catch the train into the city and see a movie.

Why do I like the quiet life? Well, I'll let you in on a secret. My parents were strict religious types, real fundamentalist arseholes, my brother and I spent our whole lives wanting to escape. He was older, so he got out first. He was a bit of a wild one, got into drugs and whatnot, turned up dead at a party one night. I've never forgotten that lesson. The wild life is not for me.

No, definitely not for me, give me a lazy Sunday arvo and I'm happy as a pig in shit. Never seen the appeal of drugs and all that. All I need is a cuppa, some quality tunes, a good book and the sunshine on the balcony. That's my happy place.

Women? Yeah, I've had a couple over the years. Never lasted too long. They always want more I find, more money, more attention, more going out, I'm content with my little slice of life, I don't want much more. Women can't be content with a simple life, that's the secret I've learned. That's why married blokes are always working like dogs to buy houses, cars, holidays and all that sort of shit. If you can learn to live without women, you'll find you don't need to work as hard and can cruise through life a bit more.

I did have one woman nearly get me on the hook. Nearly fifteen years ago now. Her name was Karen. We had a good thing going for a while. She was one of the few women, one of the few people full stop really, whom I didn't mind spending a lot of time with. We got pretty serious. She managed to fill my head with ideas about getting married and having a career. She noticed that I read a lot of books about military history and whatnot, I enjoy that sort of thing. Well anyway, she talks me into applying for the Air Force. Took me down to the recruitment centre and got me interested in a job in the logistics side of things.

I ran with it for a while. I read all the brochures they gave me and got quite interested. Seemed like a doable thing to have a career in the military and marry Karen. I could see a future all laid out for me. For a moment there I was really on board.

Well, I did all the tests and interviews and I was one week away from shipping out to basic training. Karen and I were looking through my stuff and she was telling me I had to decide what to put into storage and what to chuck out.

That was what broke the spell.

I backed out. Chickened out if you want to put it like that. I told Karen we were done. I rang the recruitment people and said that I would not be shipping out to basic training in a week as planned.

Karen cried and made a drama for a little while but when she realised I wasn't going to change my mind she faded away. I don't know where she is now. I haven't really had a girlfriend since then. Guess once you have a near miss like that it wises you up.

Funny thing, I felt really fragile, emotionally like, for ages after that. Then the routine of life took over and I settled down and felt fine. Haven't thought about Karen for years actually. In a way I kind of miss her. In a way I kind of regret not going with the Air Force thing. Oh well, life goes on, I still have my job at the bottleshop and my little flat here in Dover Court. Best to stick to the simple pleasures of life, I find. Too much ambition and fancy dreams only leads to heartache in the long run.

You've got to go? Of course, well if you ever want to pop in for a cuppa you know where I am. No need to ring ahead, I don't get out much. You can pretty much count on me enjoying the sunshine on the balcony here. Just me, watching the world go past.

TRACEY'S LAMENT

I was a bit of a dropkick when I was young.

There is no nice way of saying that so I prefer to just admit it plainly. To try and minimise it or make excuses for myself is impossible without outright lies. I prefer harsh truth to pleasant bullshit so there you have it.

I was an idle layabout and a druggie degenerate with the work ethic of a sloth and the morals of an alley cat.

This was all a long time ago and I have, of course, changed or else I wouldn't be the one telling this story.

The only excuse I can come up with that might possibly hold water is that it was the spirit of the times and I was no worse than many of my generation. It was the '90s and most people my age in Australia were bumming around not doing much. It's possible there were some who were studious and ambitious and had their eyes on careers way back then, no doubt these people will form the core of future Liberal governments, but the great majority of my peers sat around smoking cones, listening to the great music we had then and generally watched the days slip past.

You could do that back then.

The dole was a bit easier than it is now. You could sit around on it for years without too much hassle. Get yourself some friends to share a cheap rental dump and live on beans and toast and bongs. Good times.

I left high school in 1997 without a fucking clue what I was going to do with my life and no great desire to find out. I bumbled around with a couple of dead end jobs for a year but had no great love for the working life. I went on the dole shortly before my nineteenth birthday and stayed on it for three years. You could do that back then.

I was living in a share house with three other people the same age, none of them were working very hard at anything. The place was in Maylands, on Guildford Road, that whole area has been done up now but back then it was a dropkick's paradise. It suited us three just fine.

There was Tom, same age as me, same lack of drive or ambition; he supplemented his dole by doing a couple nights a week as a kitchenhand for cash in hand wages. This was before the world got completely computerised, you could still get away with that sort of thing back then.

There was Felicity. She was a beautiful girl, she looked a bit like those girls from The Corrs but with a sunburnt Australian edge to her. She had the brains and probably could have amounted to something but she liked drugs too much. It was Felicity who taught me the joys of the breakfast bong. Felicity used to wander around the house in an old dressing gown, stoned to buggery most of the time, she often had to stop and think intensely for several minutes before operating the toaster. Felicity was the first in our circle to graduate from smoking weed to harder drugs. Her end was fairly predictable even back then but that didn't make it any easier to bear when it happened.

Then there was Tracey. A short girl who looked like she would punch you in the face most of the time; she always had an air of grievance about her that I couldn't fathom, although she was easy enough to get along with. With her bobbed brunette hair and short stature, she looked like a feral Aussie version of Christina Ricci.

Tracey and I were very close, all of them were my friends but Tracey and I had something special, we were more like brother and sister than housemates. The two of us would have long and intense conversations about life, the way sensitive young people often do; we both had a sensibility that was poetic, almost spiritual, and the sharing of this became our bond.

Being unemployed layabouts we had plenty of time and very little money. We used to wander around the city talking about life. We'd browse through secondhand book stores and try to find something that was both good and cheap. We'd wander over to Northbridge and see what was happening on the street. The thing about being a druggie dropkick in the city is that your own kind can spot you and will often come up and talk to you. We had some interesting adventures and met some interesting people.

Several years drifted past like this. It's amazing how a life spent doing nothing can still feel so full. Time passed and the feeling grew in me that I should be doing something. It began to bother me to the point that I rang my cousin Doug and asked him about getting a job.

Doug was a drifter but he sneered down his nose at us because he was an employed drifter. He travelled around the country working on fishing boats, cattle stations, mine sites and roadhouses, never staying in one place longer than a year. Although he wasn't part of society any more than we were he felt himself better than us because he worked rather than claiming the dole. He had stayed at our little share house for a week when he was in between jobs and he had tried to lecture me on my life choices without much effect at the time.

Now I was ready to listen. I had begun to realise that this couldn't go on forever. The Howard government was in power at the time and had begun making noises about 'mutual obligation' and we were hearing rumours of people having their dole cut off. Time to get a job.

Doug organised jobs for the two of us on a fishing trawler based at Carnarvon. He'd done a season with these people before and told me it was a great life. I was willing to give it a go.

The day before I left Tracey and I went up to Kings Park. As if to make sure I would get homesick it was the most magnificent day in years. The sky was so blue it made me feel like I was walking through a work of art. Kings Park is an Eden overlooking the city. Tracey and I sat on the grass overlooking the CBD and watched the traffic flow across the bridges while the Australian flag fluttered from the pole in the light breeze.

Tracey sat next to me and leaned her head gently on my shoulder, the casual intimacy of people who care for each other without fanfare. She talked slowly about what the future might hold. She was unsure and dismayed that our little circle was pulling apart.

'Do you really have to go?'

Her voice was so pitiful that it broke my heart. I held her hand to reassure her.

'You know why mate, this life we're living here, it can't go on forever.'

I felt cruel as I said it. A part of me childishly wished we could just live in our little share house and do very little for the rest of our lives but I knew the harsh truth. Adulthood and real life could not be put off forever.

Tracey sighed in a quietly tragic manner and I felt awful for a few moments. The thought of causing her pain was almost enough to make me call Doug and cancel everything.

'C'mon mate, don't be like that. We're still friends, I'm only going up for a six-month season. I'll be back before you know it.'

She remained unconvinced but grudgingly accepted that I wasn't going to be talked out of it. As the afternoon faded we trudged back to the city. Between the two of us we had just enough money to get an ice cream from Macca's so we sat on a bench in the Hay Street mall and passed it back and forth between us.

The next day Doug and I were off to Carnarvon, about 800 kms to the north. We drove in his ancient Falcon station wagon taking turns at the wheel. We made it as far as Northampton on the first day and then got into Carnarvon about midday the next day.

As we drove into town the thought struck me that I had made a big mistake. The place looked like a dusty old shithole that time had passed by, the sort of place Slim Dusty would write a song about and try to romanticize. I thought about bailing out there and then and catching a bus back to Perth but I grimly held to the plan.

Once we started work I was in for a greater shock. I'd never really been to sea before and I had a moment of quiet panic when I saw the shore line recede for the first time. I had more moments of panic when we would see sharks off the side of the boat. The other men on board who were all experienced handled this very casually. They would look over the side and announce to the other blokes that there was a 'fucken Noah checking us out' and everyone would come and have a quick look. Unless the shark was really big nobody got too worried; these creatures swimming near the boat was just a fact of life.

The work was physically hard and years of being a dole bludger had made my body soft. I sweated and strained and felt pain in muscles I didn't know I had but after a while my body adjusted. Being out at sea for weeks at a time I had no access to drugs or alcohol, the hard work and heat helped sweat out whatever residues were in my system. I started to feel genuinely healthy for the first time in years.

I began to get a certain clarity of mind that I hadn't experienced before. I started to think very seriously about my life and what I was doing with it. After only two months of this life I was absolutely sure that I couldn't go back to the way I had been back in Perth.

When our time on the boat ended, Doug and I had a think about what we were going to do next. He had been in touch with someone he knew and had been offered a job at a mine site up in the Pilbara. One of the other guys on the boat was planning to go to Darwin and work on a prawn trawler based out of the harbour there, doing long stints in the Timor Sea. He had offered me a spot with him and since I was determined not to go back to Perth I said yes.

Arriving in Darwin was like landing in a foreign country. The place was so exotic compared to the suburbs of Perth. Carnarvon had been a bit of a culture shock but Darwin took that several levels further.

The work on the boat was much the same as it had been in Carnarvon except that we sometimes saw crocodiles off the side of the boat as well as sharks. I got into the rhythm of the prawn season quick enough and sweated for my money on that boat.

I had made up my mind that once the season was over, I would get some sort of normal job on land. It took about three days of looking around Darwin and I had a job at a tyre place fitting and repairing tyres. The money was okay but nothing spectacular, and the work was fairly routine once you got the hang of it. I got a little flat in Darwin and began to get domesticated, I bought furniture for the first time in my life and actually enrolled to vote. It wasn't such a bad life.

I began to feel like things were going to work out more or less okay. Like I was normal or something. I met a woman named Jackie who was a nurse at the local hospital. We hit it off, not in some exciting, passionate way, it was more like we just felt comfortable with each other. She began to come around my flat for dinner, drinks and a movie. Then she started staying the night. A few months later she moved in with me. It was nice. For the first time in my adult life I began to feel settled and comfortable.

Then Felicity died.

I got an hysterical phone call from Tracey one afternoon. It took nearly half an hour for her to come out with the details in between all the crying. She had found Felicity on the couch. At first she thought she was asleep and hadn't bothered her. Then she noticed the small trail of vomit running down the side of her face. She had checked for a pulse and hadn't found one. She had called an ambulance but it was already too late. Felicity was pronounced dead on arrival. Cause of death was a combination of valium and alcohol.

I made arrangements with my boss to take a couple of days off so I could go back down to Perth for the funeral. I told Jackie that an old friend had died but some instinct told me not to give her all the details. I had faked normality well enough and I had no wish to tell her about my dubious past.

I flew into Perth and stayed at a hotel in the city. I met with Tracey the day I arrived. She looked awful. Partly it was grief and shock, I don't think she'd slept much or stopped crying since Felicity had died, but partly it was the drugs and lifestyle. I'd been away for nearly two years and hadn't touched drugs in that time, I barely even drank anymore, so I had become healthy by default and without even realising it. Tracey on the other hand had continued down the road of drink and drugs and it was taking a toll on her body and mind.

There was a vagueness to her face, as if she had trouble processing the world around her. Her hair was ratty and there were faint wrinkles around her eyes. Even her skin looked anaemic and sallow, the inevitable result of living off beans and toast for years.

I sat her down at the nearest little café and got us both a big feed of bacon, eggs and mushrooms, not because I was particularly hungry but it seemed like a practical thing I could do to help my poor helpless friend. In between mouthfuls she told me the details of how Felicity had died.

I listened numbly as she recounted her tale of finding Felicity on the couch. On some level I'd always known Felicity was likely to die like this. Her love of drugs had always been intense and reckless, but I found it hard to imagine that she was really gone for good. I would never see her again.

I asked how Tom was taking it and was surprised to hear he had left as well. Apparently he had just walked out of the house a few days after Felicity's death. He'd left all his stuff in his room, hadn't even taken his wallet. Tracey had filed a missing person's report with the police but so far there had been no sight of him.

Tracey sat there contemplating the crumbling world around her and cried quietly. I felt like shit but couldn't see what I could do about the situation. Felicity was going to be buried tomorrow, Tom could be anywhere and I privately thought his body would be found in the river eventually. There was no comforting Tracey.

I had already made up my mind that this was going to be my last visit to my old life. I had made the break and built something for myself in Darwin. I wasn't coming back to hold the hand of a heartbroken girl regardless of our history together.

We went to the funeral the next day. There wasn't much to it. Felicity's parents had come the two hundred or so kms from Harvey for it; they glared at Tracey and me the whole time; as if blaming us for their daughter's death. I drank with Tracey that evening and we talked about old times. I felt that old warmth that I used to feel when we were together. It felt good, really good, but not good enough to keep me.

Tracey was devastated when I left the next day. She kept pleading with me to stay but I told her firmly that I had my life in Darwin now. Tom still hadn't shown up and I privately thought he never would. Tracey would be alone now. Sure she'd find some other flatmates to move in and smoke and drink with them but it wouldn't be the same.

I caught my plane back to Darwin and tried to forget it all. It didn't take long. Jackie and I were fairly happy together, my job was going well and life was good. Over the next couple of years things got even better. The tyre place I worked at was bought out by one of the big national chains, I was made manager, Jackie and I got married and started a family. I was living the great Australian suburban dream. You would never know from looking at me that I had once been a druggie dropkick.

I lost contact with Tracey. I made no effort to keep in touch and her life was so dysfunctional and chaotic that she couldn't manage to keep hold of my phone number or email address. It suited me fine. I'd been promoted to regional manager, responsible for several stores in the Darwin area and had two daughters to look after. I didn't have the time or the inclination to keep in touch with a drug addict girl in Perth.

It was twelve years after Felicity died before I set foot in Perth again. The national chain of tyre stores I worked for had organised for all the regional managers to meet in Perth for a conference and training. I'd grown used to this sort of corporate bullshit over the years and I saw it as an opportunity to get away from the missus and kids for a few days, enjoy some drinking with the other blokes, maybe even get a hooker on the quiet. What happens at corporate conferences stays there.

The first day was fairly tedious. Sales figures, marketing strategies and all that shit. I was walking back to my hotel from the conference centre thinking to myself that I should ring my wife and kids early so that I would be free to go out and drink or get a hooker later.

I had almost reached my hotel when I saw her. She was sitting on the side of the footpath with another girl, they both looked ragged and they had a small cardboard sign asking for any spare change. Passers-by ignored them both and they had a worn out, bedraggled look on their faces. I stopped and knelt down to get a better look. It was definitely her.

'Tracey, do you remember me?'

She stared at me and then something clicked and a memory emerged through the drug addled remains of her brain.

'You left us, you left me, why didn't you stay?'

She said it softly, plaintively at first.

'You left us, you left me, why didn't you stay'

'You left me, why didn't you stay?'

'You just left! How could you leave?'

The volume rising as she spoke. Now passers-by were taking an interest. I panicked. Without thinking I took a fifty dollar note out of my wallet and slammed it in front of her pathetic little cardboard sign.

'You left us!'

I walked off as fast as I could without running.

COMINGS AND GOINGS

The Senior Detective parked the car across the street and tried to make it look casual. He did fairly well, even finding some shade. He settled in for a long wait and advised his young colleague to do the same.

'Could be hours before she shows up, if she shows up, best to get comfortable I reckon.'

The younger detective nodded but wanted to ask questions. 'So, what's this place then?'

The Senior Detective hesitated for a moment, unsure if he could be bothered replying, before explaining the rundown old building they were observing.

'This is Cathy's Place, used to be a backpacker joint but there got to be too many other places in Alice Springs and this was the shittiest one of the lot. Even scummy backpackers have limits so the old bird that runs the joint turned it into a boarding house for women. Cheap and nasty but slightly better than being homeless, I suppose. It's the sort of place people stay in when they first arrive in town. Mostly transient workers and assorted shitbags stay here. This won't be the last time you come here, my boy.'

He gave a small, slightly bitter laugh, as though the never-ending workload of the Police in Alice Springs amused him. The younger Detective frowned and asked another question.

'If it's known to be full of shitbags and trouble why doesn't it get closed down? Surely if the local Commander went to the Council and showed how often we end up out here, they'd take the old girl's licence off her or something?'

The older man laughed at his common sense.

'You don't realise how this town works do you? The old bag that runs this place is proper local, been here all her life, she's probably related to half the town council and knows the other half. Not to mention that this town needs the transient workers and drifters that stay here to keep everything running. Every business in town needs workers from elsewhere or they'd shut down. There just aren't enough locals to keep the shops and pubs staffed, at least there isn't enough locals who can show up to work on time and sober. That bit is always tricky. This place serves a purpose for the town, we're just here to mop up troublemakers.'

They sat in silence for a few minutes while the younger man digested this perspective. After a few minutes, the older man pointed out a woman walking down the street towards the boarding house.

'This girl here came to town just over a month ago, she's working at the Todd Tavern now, did a check on her and ran her name through the computer the other day. Turns out she has a record down in Victoria, mostly small drugs charges and a little petty theft to support her habits, did one of those court ordered rehab things they do down there to avoid going to gaol last time. She did four of the six months she was supposed to do and then did a runner up here. If we wanted to we could lock her up and send her back to Melbourne.'

'So why don't we?' the Junior Detective asked, as if it was obvious.

'Why? She hasn't done anything up here, as far as I can tell she's clean and she's got a legit job. No, I say let sleeping dogs lie. Maybe she'll make a go of life up here, a proper second chance; I say give her the benefit of the doubt for now.'

The younger man couldn't see a good argument against this, so he said nothing. They watched the street for a little longer. A woman emerged from the boarding house, she was older, maybe fifty or so, decrepit in that way that women get when they have the misfortune to be both old and poor. Her greying hair straggled all directions out of her rather battered looking head. She wore a cardigan despite the heat and a faded old tartan skirt that might have looked okay had it not been moth eaten and stained. She bumbled rather than walked and she seemed to find daylight and the outside world a bit of a struggle.

The Senior Detective chuckled a little when he saw her. The younger man raised an enquiring eyebrow and the older man began to explain.

'That's Tabitha Holland, she's been around for years. Proper nut job. I didn't realise she was still living in this shithole. She got kicked out of her last place for being a filthy hoarder, had like five years of accumulated crap in this tiny room. She arrived in town about ten years ago on a Greyhound Bus, most people don't know this, but she's related to big money down south. Has a trust fund worth millions that she lives on. Her family own serious real estate in Sydney.'

The Junior Detective felt compelled to ask the obvious question.

'So, how'd she end up here?'

'They all end up here mate, the drifters and dropkicks of Australia, sooner or later they end up in Alice Springs. Some of them never leave. This one, I don't know what made her get on a Greyhound Bus and come here but she's still as lost as she was in Sydney. Harmless, but completely lost.'

His voice drifted away, as though lost in reverie, his eyes focused in the general direction of the old woman without actually looking at her. He snapped out of it with a start and finished his story.

'Anyway, she wanders around town, talks all sorts of off tap shit to herself, bit weird but she's never caused any trouble, so we leave her be.'

They sat for a while longer as the old woman drifted off down the street. Nothing else happened for a solid half hour and they started to get twitchy, the need to move, to do something, anything, became urgent. Eventually the younger man suggested a junk food run to the nearby shop.

'Yeah, grab me a sausage roll while you're there, Diet Coke if they have it, I'm supposed to be off the sugar according to the wife.' The older man gave instructions but made no sign of moving or reaching for his wallet. The younger man headed off to the shop without protest.

When he came back the older man was absorbed watching a man and woman outside the boarding house. For a second he thought they had got lucky and spotted their target, but his hopes were dashed.

'Yeah, nah, that bloke there is a proper sleazebag, real rockhopper, been trying to get him for ages but he's careful.'

'Boss, what's a rockhopper?'

'Old NT word, it's what the locals call drifters that come up here from down south. People with no roots, people who can't or won't settle down. Plenty of them around the place. This one here, came up nearly three years ago, been away and come back a couple of times, finds a job while he's here, then starts making connections in the drug scene, finds a silly young woman to follow him around and the whole thing ends in tears while he bolts back down south for a couple of months. He's been luckier than most, but I'll have him sooner or later. We'll see how clever he is when he's doing time in a Territory Prison, the cunt.'

They watched intently as the man talked to a woman significantly younger than himself out the front of the boarding house. They noted the absorbed, slightly adoring and devoted, way she looked at him and concluded this was his latest girlfriend/patsy.

The pair talked a little while longer and after kissing her on the cheek the man walked off down the street. For a moment they debated following him but remembering that they were here to look for their target, they stayed put.

'Remember his face, keep your eyes out for him around town, he couldn't lie straight in bed that one, sooner or later we'll get him.'

The young man nodded, his colleague's obsession worried him a little, but he didn't feel qualified to question it yet having only just made detective.

The sun rose higher and hotter in the sky, a group of Aboriginal kids came by, some on foot, some on bikes, they clocked the two men in the car as Police and started giving them cheek from across the road. A call came across the radio, their quarry had been found and arrested in another part of town, they were to come back to the station. The Senior Detective sighed wearily and started the car.

'Well, that's a couple hours of your life you'll never get back, isn't it? Still, we got to see some faces, get a sniff of what's going on in the streets, it's all about the comings and goings my boy, all about the comings and goings.'

RAIN ON THE HIGHWAY

I stayed at the Penong Caravan Park in my little tent. It was fairly quiet and I managed to get a campsite away from everyone else for the night. I slept soundly until about four in the morning when the rain started. Heavy drops on the tent sounded like drumbeats from some primeval jungle. I woke and decided to get going.

I packed and went to the roadhouse for fuel and coffee. The sun hadn't quite risen and the rain was getting heavier. I headed west and put some music on, The Cure because it seemed to match the grim sky. I had the highway mostly to myself for the first hour or so.

The sun was peeking over the horizon by the time I passed through Nundroo and when I crossed the dog fence near Yalata it was proper daylight, albeit daylight obscured by rain clouds. I got sloshed with water every time a truck went past and I started to slow down and worry about visibility. I reached Nullarbor Roadhouse at about seven and stopped to have a proper breakfast.

The sorry excuse for a carpark was covered in water and the potholes were hidden under muddy lakes. By the time I found a spot to park the bottom half of the car was covered in mud. I walked mud into their shop and ordered some breakfast and more coffee. The girl behind the counter sniffed and took my money in sullen silence as if life was an intolerable burden for her.

I sat down and ran my hand through my wet hair. The TV in the corner of the dining area was on and I stopped eating and paid attention to the weather report. Apparently this rain was part of a front coming in over WA from the Indian Ocean. The rain would be heavy and last for a couple of days. I had three days to get to Perth and I resigned myself to driving through the rain for the entirety of that time. I visualised the roads ahead of me covered in rain.

The thought occurred to me that I would have to drive slower than normal because of the shitty weather. I realised I'd only brought four CDs with me in the car and it now seemed inadequate for the trip. I browsed the selection the roadhouse had for sale in a little cardboard stand. It was a bit grim, mostly country music or golden oldies so I settled on The Eagles Greatest Hits and The Best of Rod Stewart for lack of anything better.

I set off again and slotted in the Eagles CD. The tunes were relaxing and the rain didn't get too heavy so I made good time and kept my spirits up. I passed several caravans and took risks doing so, overtaking in limited visibility, because I was unwilling to stay stuck behind them. Go be old and slow somewhere else I muttered, as I overtook them.

A gap in the rain occurred and the sun came out for about fifteen minutes, promising a glorious day of sunshine ahead. Then the rain kicked back in with a vengeance as if to mock the brief moment of sunshine. It battered down on the roof of my car as though it was expressing hatred towards me personally. I slowed right down and the windscreen wipers were going flat out trying to cope with the deluge.

About fifty kms from the border the rain eased up and I pulled into a rest area. I stretched my legs and felt some satisfying cracks and creaks from my middle-aged man's body. I walked over to the nearest bush for a piss and while I was standing there I saw a group of rabbits about twenty metres away in the scrub. They appeared to be fooling around, playing with each other and they had an air of joy about them that I found fascinating. They were reacting to the rain the same way a farmer who has survived several years of drought might, with utterly unashamed joy.

I stood there and watched them bounce around and play with each other for several minutes and felt very happy for them. Good for you little bunnies, I thought, enjoy life while you can. I turned to walk back to the car and they must have heard me because they ran back down their burrow.

I changed CDs in the car before setting off and listened to the Rod Stewart compilation as I drove across the border and down onto the Roe Plains. The rain never actually fully stopped but lightened to a mild drizzle for half an hour or so before dumping the entire Indian Ocean on the plains. I could almost watch as the dust on the plain was transformed into baby shit mud by the pouring rain. If anyone was out there beyond view of the highway on some dirt track they weren't going anywhere anytime soon.

I stopped in at Mundrabilla and thought about calling it a day. I was tired and the rain was sapping my morale, besides which it was getting dangerous with all this water on the road. I got a coffee and walked around in the drizzle stretching my legs and having a look. The motel rooms looked pretty crappy from the outside so it was a safe bet they weren't great inside. I still had plenty of driving to do before getting to Perth so I decided I would at least get to Madura today before pulling up for the night.

I got back on the highway and immediately regretted it. The trucks seemed to have increased in number and every time I passed one I was temporarily blinded by the spray. The sky was grey and miserable to match my mood. I'm definitely stopping at Madura, I decided, and hoped like hell I would make it there.

It took nearly two hours for what should have been an hour-long drive but I got there in one piece and checked in. I had a shower and let the hot water soak me thoroughly before heading to the bar.

There was a girl at the bar, real country looking; from the way she was speaking to the roadhouse staff I assumed she was local. I listened in casually for lack of anything better to do. The girl was full country, she had that proper 'Strayan' drawl that you only hear out in the bush, her clothes were rough and covered in dirt. She had that very country habit of adding 'Yeah, nah' at the beginning of every sentence. So when she spoke it was like:

'Yeah, nah, I'll just grab a coffee if I can, mate.'

'Yeah, nah, the roads are washed out so I'm stuck here for at least one day.'

I found it strangely charming.

I learned from listening in that she was named Rebecca and she lived and worked at the nearby sheep station. She had been out checking fences when the rain hit and now the tracks were so washed out she couldn't get back to the homestead and would have to stay at the roadhouse for at least one night.

I looked at her from across the bar. Her hair was dusty and brown, kept under a cap with the name of some trucking company on it. She had freckles but not too many and she wore an old flannel shirt and King Gee pants that were covered in dirt. Above the top of her belt I could just make out some underwear, not sexy, girly lingerie like you might find on a city girl but sturdy granny panties from Best and Less or somewhere similar. It made sense I thought, a girl like this who lives and works on a sheep station has no use for frilly nonsense when it comes to underwear, bog standard granny panties from Best and Less would be ideal. I forced myself to look away in case I got caught looking at her panty line but I thought about it for some time afterwards.

I ordered some food and another beer and while I ate I listened in to her conversation with the girl behind the bar.

'Yeah, nah, the northern fence line is rooted, camels keep coming down from further north and smashing it and then the dogs get in and get at the sheep. I was almost done fixing it up when this rain kicked in. Yeah, nah, stuck now and will be for a while I reckon.'

I let my imagination wander and thought about what this girl's life was like out here. Roaming about on these great open plains fixing fences and mustering sheep, hard work for sure but to be out under these open skies every day! I thought about my life, living in a concrete box called a flat in the city and commuting to another concrete box called an office every day. The bulk of my wages going on rent for the concrete box and barely having a glimpse of the sky.

I felt great anger for a moment. I'd been conned. All my life I'd been told to aim for the white-collar dream, get an education they said, work your way up the corporate ladder they said, you'll be a success they said. Yet looking at Rebecca I could tell she'd never followed any of this advice. From the way she talked I doubt if she had more than a basic high school education, I'm guessing she had no computer skills or marketing experience like I had, living out here I doubt she had much opportunity for networking or professional development. Yet she got to see the sky every day while I spent my time in concrete boxes.

I thought about this some more and had a few more beers. I watched and listened to her talk to the roadhouse staff and I couldn't help noticing the free and easy way she had about life and herself. The inconvenience of tracks being washed out and having to stay at the roadhouse was probably the worst thing that had happened to her in months. So what? She would get back to fixing the northern fence line when the rain stopped. It wasn't a big deal. I compared that to the epic shitfight that my managers had when a project wasn't done on time.

I wobbled back to my motel room and flaked out almost instantly once I hit the bed. I felt a slow burning anger at my life in the city. I also remember feeling a great surge of desire for this country girl and her granny panties. If I had been less drunk I would have had a wank in my room.

I woke in the morning and went up to the roadhouse to get coffee and breakfast. A different girl was working the counter but Rebecca was there again. She'd had a shower and her wet hair was lumped under her truckie cap like an unruly mop. She wore a faded pair of jeans and I caught a glimpse of granny panties again, presumably a clean pair.

I drank my coffee and ate my bacon and eggs and felt alive again. On a whim I spoke to her as she sipped her own coffee.

'So this sheep station you work at, how would someone go about getting a job there? Do you need to go to agricultural college or something?'

She looked at me a little surprised. Presumably this wasn't a question she was asked often, and thought about it for a second.

'Yeah, nah, just ring up the boss and ask for a job. You need a driver's licence but that's about it. It's hard work though. Yeah, nah, don't bother ringing if you're a sook.'

I thanked her and continued my breakfast while she stared at me quizzically. I finished and got in the car to head off back to my concrete box. I slipped The Cure CD on and drove off already thinking about the phone call I was going to make and how I would word my resignation letter. The rain eased off and 'Pictures of You' filled the car and my heart filled with joy. I was going to be free soon. For the first time in years I would enjoy life. It was so close I could almost taste it.

CHRISTMAS IN ALICE SPRINGS

The heat. The unstoppable, unendurable heat. Baking the ground until the red dirt is as hard as granite, wilting the trees and making the birds pant. There is barely anyone on the street to see the air shimmer from the heat. A car cruises down the highway maybe every half hour or so. Anyone with any sense is inside with the air conditioning turned up.

Just off Gap Road a woman named Carla wakes up to the sound of her children. She peels herself slowly off the bed, still sore, and walks to the lounge room to see them. The house she lives in is housing commission, built of Besser Blocks, shaped like a shoebox and with about as much charm. The inside is bare, spartan, not through choice but through poverty.

Her children are already opening the few presents she got them, cheap plastic toys from Mad Harry's mostly, their enthusiasm not diminished by the cheapness of the presents. She struggles with so much energy and noise. She really doesn't feel up to this but because it's Christmas she feels she has to refrain from yelling at them to shut up.

She makes them all a bowl of cereal each. It's supermarket brand cereal, the cheapest she could buy, the milk is also supermarket brand UHT stuff. The kids don't know any difference, so they don't complain. She turns the TV on and finds a channel playing cartoons for them. She leaves them glued to the screen and shovelling cereal in their faces and gingerly walks outside for a smoke.

There is an old plastic chair just outside the back door. This time of morning it's in the shade and somewhat pleasant. She sits down and fishes out a packet of cigarettes; she has six left. Six cigarettes for the whole fucking day. She will have to ration them out, she thinks grimly; it's going to be a miserable day as she suffers nicotine deprivation.

She smokes the first one quietly and carefully, savouring every breath. Staring out at nothing in particular on her tatty plastic throne. Her skin the colour of iced coffee except for the black around her eye. The day ahead is nothing but a burden. For a moment she feels an almost unbearable sadness for what her life is. Drawing deep on the last drag of her cigarette she stifles her self-pity with practised skill. Self-pity is a luxury as are dreams. She has to look after the kids.

Just south of the Gap there is a complex of units. They are mostly occupied by the transient workers who keep the town running without ever really being part of it. Most of the cars still have interstate plates. Everyone is from somewhere else. Christmas is a lonely time here.

A woman called Jess lives in one of the units. This is her first Christmas in Alice Springs. She is alone. Yesterday she did the obligatory phone calls to her family down south. Her Melbourne accent chatting away over several thousand kms distance, for a brief moment she felt okay. She has never not been with her family for Christmas. She didn't realize how much those simple traditions mean.

Jess lies on the bed with the air conditioner on full blast. She doesn't quite see a point in getting up and getting dressed. She's got nowhere to go, nobody to see, nothing to do, why bother?

She mopes around for several hours before finally making herself a cup of tea. She flicks on the TV and searches every channel looking for something decent. It's all shit. She thinks about streaming a movie or reading a book; it's all too much effort. She makes herself more miserable thinking about her family down south. They would be having lunch about now, maybe playing backyard cricket, her mum would be halfway through a bottle of wine by now. She misses it so much.

She only came to Alice Springs because she couldn't get a decent job in Melbourne. All those years doing her degree and she still had to work at Macca's for six months after graduating. She saw the ad online and decided that Alice Springs couldn't be that bad, it must be better than working at Macca's, she thought. She applied and got the job. She imagined a bright future for herself.

What she has is a job that pays alright but requires her to live in this shithole of a town away from everyone she cares about. She paces about her little flat like a tiger in a cage at the zoo. She decides to go and have a swim in the little pool at the far end of the complex. She gathers a towel and wanders down. The car park is so empty, it's scary. Everyone who can has gone back home for Christmas. What's left is people who can't get time off work or don't have enough money to get out of town.

She walks down the step slowly and eases herself into the water thinking it will be cold. It's warmed by the sun and is decidedly tepid. She dunks her head under and feels something approaching pleasure. A splash around, a few laps, and she starts to feel better. She rests herself against the side of the pool for a moment. Her head leans against the warm brick while her feet tread water gently. She notices the little swallows flying around like miniature jet fighters. They swoop in low over the pool and take little gulps of water as she watches.

As she watches, she becomes aware of the silence. There is nobody around, hardly any traffic to make a noise, not a single plane in the sky as far as she can see. She looks at the big red hills surrounding the town, the blue sky and its merciless sun. She feels more alone than she ever has in her life.

In the centre of town, a petrol station is open. A man named Christopher is working behind the counter; he hates being there today, but he needs the money, he wants to get out of town. He never planned to live in Alice Springs, his car broke down while he was running away from Perth and trying to get to Cairns. He lives in the cheapest dump of a boarding house he could find; he works as many shifts as he can get at the servo in order to save the money to get on the road again. It's been four months so far.

There are hardly enough customers coming through to warrant his being there. The heat makes the highway unbearable to all but the most desperate travellers, those people who really have to get somewhere no matter what.

He had been one of them only four months ago. He had to leave Perth. Years of drinking, doing drugs and burning bridges had soured things for him there. He was either going to end up in gaol or a shallow grave. He had no friends anymore.

The plan had been to get to Cairns. He'd never been there but the idea of a tropical getaway appealed to him; he thought he could maybe make some sort of life for himself there and stay permanently or else wait a year or two until the mess he'd made in Perth had blown over. Instead here he is in Alice Springs, stuck until further notice in the arsehole of Australia. Hating every minute of it. All because his shitbox car had died just south of Stuarts Well.

He mentally ran through the numbers again. He'd looked around and he could get a decent secondhand car for just over three grand. Add to that, fuel, food and accommodation until he got to Cairns, then a bit saved away in case he didn't find a job straight away once he got there. All up he reckoned he needed five grand cash sitting in the bank before he could leave. Right now, he has two grand. He had already told the boss he was willing to do every shift he could get, if anyone quit or chucked a sickie he would gladly do their shift. It helped but every week he pays rent in this town slows him down. He lives on the cheapest diet he can, he's mastered the art of the budget grocery shop, but it's still going to take time.

Maybe another three months, maybe longer, probably closer to five months, stuck in this town, stuck in this job and stuck in this heat. The thought is unbearable. He restocks the drinks fridge to take his mind off it.

The heat. The unstoppable, unendurable heat. The town bakes under it, powerless to resist, everyone who can is inside with the air conditioning flat out. In the Todd River a small group of Aboriginals sits under the little bit of shade they can find. A truck rattles through town, driving the Stuart Highway north to Darwin. Half an hour later a caravan cruises the same route in the opposite direction, an old couple heading south to Adelaide. The day passes in a haze of heat.

THE EXILE

Mary Gibson lived in an old brick house in Alice Springs. It had been built and paid for by her husband who had died five years previously of lung cancer. Ronnie Gibson had been a tradie and had made good money, enough to build and pay off the house and go on holidays to Tasmania every year. He had planned to move to Tasmania with Mary when he retired but a lifelong smoking habit caught up with him and he got a small plot in the Alice Springs cemetery instead.

Mary sat in the kitchen of her late husband's house one January morning in 2019. It was the hottest summer for a long time, and she was sipping iced water while she waited for her daughter to get ready. She was thinking about her time in this house and realised that it was almost exactly twenty-two years that she had lived here. She searched her memory and ran the numbers in her mind, twenty-three years since she arrived in Alice Springs on the old Greyhound bus, just on twenty-two years since she moved into this house with Ronnie.

She sipped her water.

She had arrived in town with a bag of clothes and about two hundred dollars to her name. She was fleeing Adelaide, her family and its limitations. She had stolen the money for her bus fare from her dad. She simply dipped into his wallet one night when he was asleep and took all the notes and left the coins. When she got to the bus ticket office she asked how far she could get with that amount of money, and the furthest place available was Alice Springs.

By such small and random decisions are our fates determined.

When she had first landed in town she was still Mary Dietrich. She had always hated her last name and was happy to change it for her husband's. Her family was an old German dynasty of South Australia, one of many rooted deep in the Adelaide Hills. She had ancestors buried all through Hahndorf and Stirling and cousins by the dozen in various dull Adelaide suburbs. Some people would have been proud of such a heritage. Some people were fuckwits in her opinion.

She had met Ronnie within a few weeks of landing in Alice Springs. She was working at the little takeaway place down Gap Road serving hot chips and cold drinks to people all day. It wasn't much of a job, but it paid her rent. Ronnie had been one of the regular tradies coming in for smoko every day. They had got friendly, he had asked her if she wanted to come to a small party on the weekend, she hadn't really made any friends in town yet, so she said yes, they started seeing each other, she got pregnant, they got married, life ran its course.

'Mum, how much time we got till we have to be at the airport?'

Mary's walk down memory lane was interrupted by her daughter Natasha.

'About an hour but it's always best to be early with these things, so get a move on.'

Natasha emerged presently and added another bag to the two that were already on the loungeroom floor.

'They're going to charge you for that you know, extra baggage and all that, these airlines don't miss a trick, you know.'

'I know but I need all this stuff.'

'Do you really? You can buy clothes once you're down there, they have shops in Melbourne, you know.'

'Yeah but I need this stuff.'

Mary dismissed it with a wave and gave up arguing. Her daughter could work out her own life apparently. She'd managed to get into a university in Melbourne without her help, she'd managed to organise a share house with some other students without her help, presumably she'd organise her luggage without her help.

As they drove to the airport Mary noticed her daughter's complete lack of sentiment. No last look at the town she had been born and raised in. No soft words for her mother, no tears, no nothing. Instead she had her phone out and was browsing Instagram photos or something.

She's a cold little bitch, Mary thought, no point expecting regular phone calls or emails, once she's gone she's really gone. She'll transform herself into a snobby little Melbourne girl and wear all the right clothes and have all the right friends and I won't hardly ever hear from her again.

Mary pictured herself in her little brick house, alone, for year after year after year, nothing much changing, nobody to care. Her son had left a few years back, Ronnie Jr had done his apprenticeship, got his trade qualifications and set off for the mines in the Pilbara to chase the big money. Not a thought for his mother on her own back in Alice Springs. Now Natasha was going, too. Mary asked herself what she had to show for her life, a dead husband, a son gone off interstate, a daughter going off interstate and a little brick house in Alice Springs. It didn't seem enough.

They arrived at the airport and went through the tedious business of checking in. As predicted they charged Natasha more for her extra stuff. Mary restrained herself from saying, I told you so.

The boarding call came, and Mary waited to see if Natasha would crack. If she would show something resembling actual human emotion.

'Bye, Mum.' A quick hug and a kiss on the cheek and it was all over. Her daughter walked away to the boarding gate with a smile on her face and not a care in the world. Eighteen years of parenting over and done with. The nest was officially empty.

For a moment Mary was unsure what to do. Wait for the plane to take off? She couldn't see what that would achieve. Go straight home? The thought was depressing beyond words, to be all alone in that little brick house hiding away from the heat in the air conditioning because there was nowhere for her to go and nothing for her to do.

In the end she grabbed a bottle of Fanta from the little airport shop and drove away from the airport back towards town but with no intention of going home just yet. She saw the cemetery up ahead and decided to pull in.

She parked the car, loose gravel crunching under the tyres, as near to the gate as she could. The last few people from an earlier funeral were leaving, awkward groups of two or three dressed in formal clothes shuffling out the gate. Mary wondered who had died; she recognised some of the people but didn't remember hearing about anyone dying.

Mary walked inside the cemetery gates. The local council did a good job with this place, she thought, it was remarkably green and pleasant given they lived in a desert and it was the middle of summer. She walked in shade most of the way to Ronnie's grave. She saw a couple of council workers over the other side doing something to a tree but aside from that she was alone now.

She sat down beside Ronnie's grave. He was in the middle of a row of a dozen or so graves bookmarked at one end by a grand old Lemon Gum and at the other by a gnarly old Olive Tree. The two trees combined to provide almost total shade cover for Ronnie Gibson's last resting place.

Ronnie's grave wasn't much to look at. A simple headstone with the relevant dates inscribed. Mary reached out and ran her hand over the granite and read the words she already knew by heart.

In Loving Memory of Ronald Gibson

3-4-1957 — 8-11-2014

Loving Husband and Father

Ronnie had chosen those words himself when the cancer diagnosis hit him. He wasn't much of a one for sentiment, he'd said, he preferred to keep bullshit to a minimum. The one really important and meaningful thing in my life, he declared, was my family, anyone could have done my job, it didn't matter, but my wife and my kids were special to me and that's the only thing I want on my headstone.

Mary had complied with his wishes and arranged everything with the funeral directors before the time came. At first it had felt ghoulish to be organising her husband's funeral while he lay in the cancer ward dying but towards the end she was glad it was done. They sent him off properly and the kids got to say goodbye in a dignified way.

Mary visited his grave regularly. Somewhere along the line she had started talking to him. She would sit and tell him things that were on her mind. She didn't know what impulse had started her talking like this but once it began she felt she needed it. Her regular trip out to the cemetery became a therapeutic necessity. As the kids grew more independent and needed her less she needed this time at Ronnie's grave more.

This day she felt more alone than ever and under the shade of the trees she began to talk as she sat in front of the stone.

'Ronnie, our girl went away today. You should see her now all grown up, she's become a right little miss, a lot like me when I was that age. I don't think she's ever coming back to Alice Springs, Ronnie. She wants the type of life you can only have in the big city. She'll probably stay in Melbourne for good now, I don't think she's the sort to reminisce or get homesick or anything like that. She's gone Ronnie, I've lost her.'

The barest hint of a sob escaped but her self-control reasserted itself.

'I'm all alone now Ronnie, our boy is off in WA chasing the big money in the mines. He forgets to email me for months at a time and then I get a pissy little message when he remembers.

I'm not holding my breath expecting emails or calls from Natasha. I don't have anyone any more. I go to work and come home to our empty house. Everything is still pretty much as you left it. I don't know what to do with myself.'

'Sometimes I wonder what it was all for, Ronnie, why did I go to all that effort just to end up here? Life plays some funny tricks, I thought getting away from my family in Adelaide was all I needed to stop the misery. I thought once I did that life would get better and I'd have more sunny days. You and I got married and had our babies and I thought, yeah life is working out okay, I did the right thing. Now it's like all that good stuff just ran out of steam. I don't know why it had to end up like this. I don't know what to do, Ronnie.'

'I was so young when I met you, Ronnie, I'd just hit eighteen, I know people used to make comments because you were older, but I never cared about that shit. You were good to me, the best, all those years we had were great. I thought I was done with unhappiness when I met you. I'd had so much misery growing up, I know I never told you the whole story of it all but that was for your benefit not mine, the horrible details would have broken your heart. I made myself think of my life as starting the day I arrived in Alice Springs on the bus. Like everything before had been a mistake. '

'Maybe this happens to everyone as they get older, but I feel like all this time has made no difference. Like I'm back where I was when I was eighteen. One of my aunties used to call it 'the Dietrich curse', she used to say our family had a darkness in them. She told me once that nobody in our family had ever died happy, that every last one of us went to our graves in sorrow and suffering. Maybe she was onto something. Maybe I'm cursed.'

'I don't know what to do Ronnie, I don't want to be alone, waiting around in our little house, in this little town, just biding time until I die. I'm only in my forties, I could still have some good years left but I don't know what to do. I can never go back to Adelaide. I still don't ever want to see my family again and anyway there's a good chance they're all dead by now. I don't know any other place really, we were always going to do the move to Tasmania when you retired but I wouldn't do it on my own, there's no point me moving there without you.'

She sighed, exhausted from speaking her feelings out loud, exhausted from the heat and exhausted from life. She ran her hands lovingly over the words inscribed on her husband's grave. With no further ceremony she stood up and brushed herself off, and walked slowly through the heat back to her car.

A hot wind blew in from the north west carrying with it the stinging heat from the Tanami Desert. Driving away from the cemetery Mary's car was buffeted, and the air conditioner worked overtime to keep things barely endurable. She had nothing to do for the rest of the day. No work until tomorrow. No kids in the house. Just the loneliness of exile and the time ticking by.

THE FAMILY FARM

He leaves Ceduna on a hot day, driving east towards Adelaide, his car stuffed with literally everything he owns in the world. Making reasonable time on the thin strip of tar which dignifies itself with the title Highway, he reaches Wirrulla and pulls into the town.

The railway tracks make his car rattle as he drives over them a little faster than he should. He parks in the main street of the tiny town, one or two little shops in the shadow of the silos, and checks his phone reception. Three bars but no messages, they should have called back by now, he thinks, and his already high level of anxiety cranks up a notch. He chews his finger-nails, a filthy habit that he only indulges when stressed.

He walks up the main street for a few minutes to stretch his legs. The town is so quiet he can hear traffic back on the highway in one direction and birds in the paddocks in the other. He looks up at the towering silos and wonders how long they've been there. Fifty years? It's a guess but he takes it as gospel for lack of better information. He feels pretty sure that nothing has happened in this town in that time. The one little shop, the falling–apart–where–it–stands pub and the dusty Post Office tell him that much. Those silos have stood there like the Australian version of the pyramids. Over a few hundred people living in the town and literally nothing even remotely exciting has happened.

He thinks about the lives the local people must live and tries to imagine the years and decades of not much happening, in this little cluster of buildings surrounded by paddocks and watched over by the silos. He compares this to the chaos of his own life, currently running from Perth and the mess he left there as fast and as far as his limited funds can take him, and thinks that maybe these people have it better than him. Briefly he lets his imagination run wild, settling in this tiny town, finding a job, maybe meeting a local girl and living a long, quiet and happy life. He imagines sitting down years from now with his kids grown up and telling them the story of how he just happened to stop here and meet their mother.

He shakes his head. If he can't get to Adelaide tonight and if his sister won't let him stay at her place for a while he is sleeping in his car for the foreseeable future. That's reality, no happy ever after in a little country town for me.

He gets back in the car and heads out to the highway again. Turns east towards Adelaide and the grim prospects of the future. The road winds a little and patches of scrub break up the farmland. Dry paddocks of wheat stubble are being slowly grazed by sheep under a sky so blue it almost hurts his eyes.

He tries to keep his mind off his troubles. He's sick of drifting through life, he's sick of running from messes in different parts of the country and more than anything else, he's sick of being broke.

He had to leave Perth in a hurry so he only has a couple of CDs in the car and he got sick of them somewhere near

Norseman. He flicks through the radio until he finds something. It's the ABC regional radio station, for lack of better options. The station is a country one so the news of markets, trade agreements and weather take priority over everything else. He hadn't known there was so much discussion to be had about beef exports to China but the radio milks almost an hour out of the subject.

He checks his phone and notices he's out of range again. A minute later he looks for a distance sign. One appears shortly and tells him that it's fifty kms from Poochera. I'll stop there, have lunch and maybe try calling again. If he has no luck it's a night sleeping in the car, maybe several nights.

The first he sees of Poochera is the silos standing sentinel over the plains. They should stop bothering to name these little towns and just call them 'Silo Town 1' and 'Silo Town 2' and so on. It would be more convenient.

He pulls in at the little roadhouse and tops up with fuel. He pays and then moves the car out of the way so he can sit in the little roadhouse café and make some phone calls while he eats a sandwich. He tries his sister again and finally gets hold of her. Turns out she had received his earlier message but didn't really want to reply. She doesn't say that of course, she's too polite, but he can tell from her voice that she really doesn't want to be having this conversation.

'What is it now?'

'Well here's the thing…' He continues, knowing he isn't convincing her. 'I just need a place to stay, only for a couple of days, I'll get in touch with the mob I worked for up in the NT, I left on good terms with them and that was less than a year ago, shouldn't be a drama to get my old job back. I'll be no trouble for you, I'll stay out of the way, I literally just need a room to crash in for three or four days at the most.'

She sighs down the phone. 'All right then'

'Cheers Sis, you're a legend.'

Inwardly he curses her for the privileged selfish bitch she is. Mum and Dad's favourite who always toed the line and never set a foot wrong. She will hold this over him for years to come and use it as ammo in family arguments whenever it suits her.

The immediate danger is passed. He got out of Perth and over the state border before they could get him. He has a place to stay while he plans his next move. Everything is going to be ok. Everything is going to be ok. Everything is going to be ok.

He sits for a while in the tacky little café and watches the slow drip of highway traffic pass. The woman at the counter idly restocks the fridge while the TV in the corner plays a midday talk show.

His mind wanders and he daydreams about life in a little town like this. Maybe he could work in this roadhouse. Live like a hermit in this little town. Refuse to ever get involved in anything remotely dodgy again. Grow old and become an old man who potters about the little town. He smiles. Once he's stable again and back earning decent cash he'll chase action again, then maybe a year or so from now he'll find himself doing a runner across the country again. That last thought sobers and depresses him. He sighs wearily, stands up and heads for the door.

The woman behind the counter looks up as he opens the door and mumbles goodbye. He pulls out onto the highway, hits the accelerator and picks up speed as he leaves the little township of Poochera.

A sudden urge to piss makes him pull off the road. He parks in front of a farm gate. He pisses on a fence post and then pauses to look around. The gate is open and there is a dirt track leading through paddocks. In the distance he can see a house and some sheds, presumably where the farmer and his family live. All harsh sunlight and empty silence of wheat paddocks as far as he can see. A sign next to the mailbox by the gate reads

Whitby Downs

T.J Whitby and sons

EST 1904

Since 1904 this family has had a place, they belong somewhere, they have roots.

He looks back at his car parked in the dust. The boot and backseat are piled high with everything he owns. He will sleep in his sister's spare room tonight and endure her resentment and a small lecture about what he's doing with his life.

He looks at the sign again. He would do just about anything to trade places with The Whitby Family. But life gets handed to you on a plate like leftovers at a soup kitchen and you have to eat it and be grateful. You don't get to choose.

He has a long way to go before he reaches Adelaide.

PEACHES IN SUMMER

'Tully, Daniel.'

The officer called his name and he stood up. He moved awkwardly, this was the first time he'd worn civilian clothes for a long time, they felt strange on his skin, they lacked the harsh rub and grime of his prison clothes.

The officer ran through something called a 'Pre-Release Checklist' with him. Bank account organized? Check. Centrelink organized? Check. Place to live organized? Check. Personal property returned to him? Check.

'Right then, sign here and we'll get you in the van and out of here. Best of luck and try not to come back.'

Daniel signed the paperwork in front of him. It was over. The ordeal was over. 3 years, 5 months and 12 days. Done. He was free now. He gathered up the small bag containing his possessions and paperwork and followed another officer to a van parked outside.

The drive into the city was overwhelming. All these people, all this space. You don't appreciate a simple thing like blue sky until you've spent 3 years, 5 months and 12 days sitting in a concrete cell looking at four walls.

The van negotiated its way through the Adelaide CBD and onto South Terrace. Daniel stared at the parklands with desperate longing. He hadn't seen that much open space and green grass in 3 years, 5 months and 12 days. Down the slightly decrepit end of South Terrace they stopped outside his new home. Terrace Lodge, a boarding house for men of slender means and dubious history. He was going to live here for the immediate future.

The officer driving the van was in no mood for hanging around and drove off the second Daniel got out. Inside, he found a grimy looking man behind a grimy looking desk.

'I've got a room booked.'

'Name?'

'Daniel Tully'

'Yeah no worries, you're written in the book, the social worker from the prison organized it all. Right, let's get you sorted.'

He explained the rules of the establishment to Daniel. Told him where things were and what to do and not do. Daniel paid him cash out of the thousand dollars they gave him when he was released. He was given a key and a receipt.

He walked to his new room. It wasn't much larger than the cell he'd been living in. The walls had probably been white at some point, but years of tobacco smoke and neglect had turned them a murky yellow-brown. There was a single bed and a couple of little drawers at one end and a large window at the other. Daniel was pleased to discover he could see the parklands from his window. He sat for a moment, there was no need to pack away his stuff, he didn't have enough to make a job of it. Instead he sat quietly and let the enormity of the moment run through him.

His life had started again. He was reborn. Born again like the Christians who used to come and hold services in the prison would say. He thought of the Jesus story, crucified and died, lay in a tomb for three days then rises from the dead. His own story was less dramatic; arrested, rotted away in a concrete box for 3 years, 5 months and 12 days and now, like a white trash Jesus, he had risen.

He sat on the edge of the single bed as the emotions threatened to overwhelm him. However, his time in prison had taught him to repress his feelings, show nothing. He beat it all down inside himself and thought about what he was going to do first. He had heard the bravado of other prisoners when they talked about the first thing they would do when they got out. Usually it involved fucking a woman or drinking a bottle of some good whiskey. If he was honest with himself, he just wanted fresh air and open space right now.

For 3 years, 5 months and 12 days he hadn't been able to walk wherever he wanted, hadn't been able to step outside when he wanted, hadn't been able to see beyond the walls and razor wire. Now he could walk across the street to the parklands with absolute impunity.

It was nearly lunchtime and there were people moving about, office workers having their break, mums taking their kids to the park, delivery drivers dodging traffic to get there on time. The sense of life, being alive and being part of the world, was intoxicating. He walked out across the grass, into the heart of the parklands. He wanted to feel the open space.

He stopped when he thought he was almost in the exact centre of a large cricket field. It was empty now but presumably would have been used on the weekends. He stood and looked around, stretched his arms out and let his head fall back, eyes looking directly upwards at the blue summer sky. He stood there embracing the sky, embracing life, inhaling the sweet-smelling parklands air. The smell of grass, the sound of birds, the gentle hum of traffic, the stink of prison slowly falling off him.

He put his arms down. He felt glorious. His face tingled with joy. He looked around the park and thought how very good it was to be free.

He decided to wander into the city and see what there was to see.

He walked up Pulteney Street, noting the things that had changed; a new shop here and there, an old shop no longer there, and those that hadn't. His eyes took in the people walking around, the people sitting and eating at the pub as he walked past. His brain struggled to process it all. His stomach growled and he thought intensely about what his first post-prison meal should be. The food they had been served inside was shit, instant mashed spuds out of a tin, grim stews that were more greasy water than meat and veg, it kept you alive but seemed to be designed by sadists to make your existence even more horrible. He had fantasied about his first meal outside for a long time. Sometimes he thought of getting a big old-fashioned pub parmi with chips and a big cold beer. Other times he thought about Chinese or a proper steak with gravy dripping off it.

He had made it to Rundle Mall and there were people every-where. For a moment he felt confused until he remembered the food court in the Myer Centre. That would do for now.

He rode the escalators, his first in 3 years, 5 months and 12 days, and scanned around. He saw the Chinese place, one of those bog-standard food court joints that serve three choices with rice or noodles for ten bucks. He realized he was staring and with an effort he composed himself before walking over and ordering.

Honey Chicken had never tasted so good. Not for 3 years, 5 months and 12 days. It was divine, orgasmic almost, all that grimy prison food was now a distant memory. He had reached a higher plane of existence where a man could kiss an angel and her lips would taste like Honey Chicken.

Nobody else in the food court seemed to be having the same intense experience with their food that he was; they rushed and ate quickly, in a hurry to get back to work, or they ate and talked, the food being a mere background to their social interaction. They had no idea of the subtle joys he was experiencing over here.

He spent the rest of the afternoon wandering around the city. He needed some new clothes, so he got a couple things from Kmart, he remembered there was no TV in his new room, so he hit up Dymocks for something to read. As the day dragged on the excitement of it all made him fatigued.

He went to Woolworths to get some basic groceries, something to eat tonight and tomorrow morning. He was out of practice with the whole grocery buying business but as he wandered around the aisles it started coming back to him.

He stopped in one aisle and looked at a tin on the shelf. Peaches. He hadn't had peaches in a long time, even before he went to prison, not since he was a kid really. A memory came to him, the summer days when they'd all gone to the beach. When they got home Mum would make them a bowl of peaches and vanilla ice cream each, they would sit cross legged on the carpet and eat while they watched videos.

Long suppressed emotions began to bubble up. He forced the emotions down, he had a lot of practice at not feeling things that were awkward, he forced himself to move. He took the tin of peaches from the shelf, found the ice cream aisle and grabbed himself a tub of vanilla, went through the checkout as fast as he could.

His legs marched him all the way back to the boarding house without too much conscious thought on his behalf. He made it to his room without cracking up and locked the door behind him. He found the least chipped bowl and the least bent spoon and poured in the peaches, syrup and all. He dug out several generous scoops of ice cream and placed it on top of the peaches like decorations on a wedding cake. He looked at it for a moment, remembering years gone by and wrong turns taken.

Very slowly, as slow as a surgeon operating on a man's heart, he dipped his spoon in and brought it to his mouth. He tasted. And felt that life was very good indeed.

THE PROBATIONARY
CONSTABLE

'Chuck the lights on and gun it!'

His Sergeant's command rang in his ears as he sped down the highway south of Alice Springs. The patrol car responded well, and they were hitting 140 kms within a few seconds. They sped past the turn off to Pine Gap, past the prison, out onto the open Stuart Highway towards where the call had come from.

Truck collision with a car, multiple fatalities and multiple injuries, ambulance required urgently. The radio call was fast and desperate. They had reacted with haste.

It came into view, he heard his Sergeant mutter 'fuck!' quietly as he saw it, a truck, a full-blown road train no less, had slammed into the side of a backpacker's van as it pulled out of a rest area. It looked bad. There were going to be deaths here, they both knew this before they even stepped out of the patrol car.

'They just came out of nowhere, I couldn't stop in time.'

The truck driver offered his pitiful explanation as they approached, still holding the Sat-phone he'd used to call 000.

'They just came out of nowhere, I couldn't stop in time.'

They inspected the wreck; two young men on the driver's side were dead, they'd copped the brunt of the impact and it had made a mess of them. No point even trying to help them. A girl in the front passenger seat had badly knocked her head against the window. The Sergeant checked for a pulse, nothing.

They checked the girl in the rear passenger side, put his finger on her throat, there was a pulse, finally something good. The Ambulance officers came and assisted them in getting her out.

She moaned as they moved her. Sarge tried to talk to her.

'What's your name, sweetheart?'

A confused mumble from the blood streaked face.

'Can you say that again? What's your name?'

'Francesca'

'Ok Francesca, where are you from?'

'Italia'

'Ok Francesca from Italia, I'm Sergeant Matthews of the Northern Territory Police. You've been in a bad accident. We're going to take you to hospital now. Ok?'

'My friends?'

The question was desperate and pitiful.

'They're going to hospital too, they'll be in the other ambulance, you're going to be okay Francesca.'

The lie rolled so smoothly that the poor girl never questioned it. The ambulance officers rushed off, lights blaring, hoping to make it to the hospital in town in time.

A gathering of uniforms and vehicles was underway. Each vehicle, police and ambulance, had its emergency lights flashing.

As if they could get the situation under control by force of illumination. As if the crisis would abate if you acknowledged it was a crisis and took it seriously enough.

'Go talk to the truckie, make him blow in the bag and get a statement from him,' the Sergeant barked.

The young Constable focused on the task at hand. He took a breathalyser from the patrol car and walked to where the truckie stood.

'Mate, I just need you to blow into this for me.'

The truckie blew zero, this bloke was stone cold sober, thought the young Constable.

He asked the truckie to tell him what happened.

'They just pulled out mate, like they didn't even look, I couldn't do anything. I slammed on the brakes, but it was too late.'

He paused and ran his hand through his thinning hair. A look of despair crossed his face, his lip quivered for a second and the young Constable thought he was going to cry.

'This is the second fucking time this has happened to me. I'm careful, I do everything I can to be safe, but sometimes it just happens anyway. People slip up once, they don't look, and I can't stop my truck quick enough, boom, all over. Fuck me.'

He finished his emotional outburst and pulled a pack of cigarettes from his pocket. He lit one with shaking hands and sucked the smoke down like a shell-shocked soldier.

Higher ranking officers had arrived on the scene. A Police photographer was snapping pictures of the dead bodies and the wrecks. Traffic was being directed around the carnage. The situation was officially under control.

'Truckie blew zero Sarge, reckons the backpacker van just pulled out and he had no time to stop.'

'I figured as much, look at the skid marks from the truck, he's slammed the brakes on hard trying to stop but it was too late. No skid marks from the van, they probably didn't look, might not have even seen it until it hit them. They forgot to look both ways this one time and that's it, one little mistake and they'll never see home again.'

'You can get angry at the stupid kids for not being more careful, but it doesn't help. Mistakes happen and sometimes they're fatal. All anyone can do is try not to fuck up but there is no certainty in life.'

The Sergeant gazed off into the distance. The sun was starting to drift towards the horizon across the empty miles of red dirt and scrub to the west.

'Their families back in Europe will get a knock on the door from the local Police in the next few days.'

The young Constable looked around at the scene, the dead bodies covered by blankets in the crumpled van, the truck driver talking to another officer, his face full of grief and despair.

He remembered the feeling he'd had when he marched in his graduation parade at the academy. He remembered his parents taking photos with him in his shiny new uniform.

The van from the mortuary pulled up and a jovial fat fellow got out.

'Where do you blokes want me to park? Oh, can I get one of you to give me a hand lifting them in the van? My offsider chucked a fucking sickie on me today. Always the way isn't it?

Thousands of unemployed people in this country and I'm stuck with a Muppet for an offsider.'

The young Constable looked off into the dusty distance again for a moment.

'Yeah, no worries, I'll give you a hand.'

THE MUNDRABILLA SUICIDE

I was living and working at Madura Roadhouse a few years back. The isolation of roadhouse work suited me fine. I worked my shift during the day, retired to my room in the staff quarters and read books and the real world didn't even touch me.

To keep myself at least a little bit fit I started walking in the bush around the roadhouse. Over time I started taking an interest in the wildlife I was seeing out there, I got myself a field guide to Australian birds and a book about Australian reptiles so I could identify what I was seeing.

It's easy to lose yourself when you're working remote, you go out there with the intention of doing six months, saving some money and getting yourself stabilized while you work out what to do next, then a year passes, the outside world becomes a mildly amusing spectacle on TV, if you even have TV, then before you know it two years have gone by and you're still in the middle of nowhere but you've grown comfortable with it. Sporadic short visits to the city convince you that civilization is overrated and you learn to love the emptiness of the plains with almost religious devotion.

I was pretty much at this point when it happened. I'd lost interest in returning to the real world and had begun to despise it. I couldn't imagine living without being able to walk out onto the Roe Plains and see from horizon to horizon with not a soul in sight.

It was Bustards that got me. The Australian Bustard (Ardeotis australis) also known as a Bush Turkey or Plain Wanderer. Fairly rare these days but I saw some on the Roe Plains and got hooked on spotting them. I started searching further afield to catch sight of them, taking old sheep station tracks that were almost grown over and spending hours in the middle of vast empty saltbush plain beyond the reach of the modern world.

I was following an old track that hadn't been used for years, maybe 30 kms west of Mundrabilla, half grown over with scrub but still visible and drivable, just. I stopped the car near a clump of scrubby Mulga tress surrounded by knee-high saltbush that stretched off into the distance. Experience had taught me that wildlife used these irregular clumps of thicker scrub as shelter so if I was going to see anything it would likely be there.

I walked quietly towards the copse, eyes peeled for movement when I saw something blue and boxy. Looking closer I realized it was a car. What was a car doing out here so far from anything? It was abandoned, grass had grown up around the back tyre and there was a thin coating of dust and leaves on the roof.

I stopped dead in my tracks, I looked around, suspicious that I was being watched but I was as alone and isolated as it is possible to be in the modern world. I came up along the driver's side and I saw him. A corpse, decayed almost beyond recognition, sitting in the driver's seat, skin stretched over bones like ancient parchment, clothes worn and tatty, a mangy rug of hair still holding the fort on top of his skull like the last raggedy survivor of a battle. I froze, eyes and ears strained to hear whoever was stalking me. After a few minutes I relaxed and began to look closer.

He was maybe my height, medium build I suppose, nothing remarkable about him physically other than the fact he was dead and half rotted away. His clothes looked distinctly cheap even if they hadn't been dressing a corpse, grubby jeans, basic sneakers and a flannel shirt, classic poor Bogan wear. His left sleeve looked like it had been rolled up and amongst what remained of his skin and tissue I could just barely see the top of a syringe.

There was a pile of paper on the passenger seat, like one of those cheap notebooks you can get at a newsagent. Had he been writing the greatest book ever written in this country before he died, a masterpiece which would finally put Australia on the literary map but now no one would ever read it? I smiled as I stood peering into the car window, amused by my own gallows humour, and thought about what I was going to do.

I checked my phone and saw no reception but I knew if I drove back out to the highway I would get maybe two bars. Calling the Eucla cops seemed like the best idea so I went with that. As I walked towards my own vehicle the feeling of being watched came over me again and I paused and looked around for a few minutes. The saltbush plain stretching out into nothing was entirely deserted except for myself. I heard my own breathing and the faintest whisper of wind; I wanted to run but stayed calm and walked slowly back to my own car.

I followed the overgrown dirt track back out to the highway without incident. I parked myself just off the verge and rang the

Eucla police station. A lone truck passed by while I was waiting for someone to pick up. I could hear its engine fading into the distance, discreetly folding itself back in the overpowering silence of the plain as if it had never passed by at all. Eventually someone answered the phone and I explained what I had found.

When the cops got there it was the old salty veteran Sergeant all the locals and long timers on the highway nicknamed 'Dicky Knee', like the puppet from that old TV show. I don't know why he acquired this name but he was an alright bloke, totally allergic to work though, constantly finding new and creative methods to bludge out of sight of his superior officers. The other officer with him was a new bloke, obviously from the city and finding bush policing a bit challenging.

When I explained what I'd discovered to them I could see Dicky Knee's heart sink; he knew this meant a lot of paperwork, dead bodies can't be ignored. We headed back off the highway and down the barely visible track. We stopped and I walked them to the car in the scrub.

'Fuck me, this bloke's been dead at least a year, maybe two, what the fuck are we supposed to do with the cunt? Obviously no one gives a shit if he's been out here this long, why didn't you just leave him be?' Dicky Knee ranted. I could see his mind running through what had to happen now and the work he wouldn't be able to avoid, as if the prospect horrified him. He began to mutter to himself.

'Fuck.'

'Fucken fucker.'

'Fucking useless dead cunt.'

'There's gonna be a mountain of fucking paperwork for this cunt.'

And so on…

After ten minutes he made a decision.

'Right, young fella, you stay here while we go back to the Highway and make some calls. This whole fucking thing is a crime scene until further notice. The forensics mob will have to come down from Kalgoorlie. Fuck me.'

I followed him out to the highway and waited while he made the call. He grimaced; obviously this was a big deal and bludging out of sight of the boss for the rest of the day was out of the question.

'You'll have to make a statement saying what you saw and did and all that sort of thing,' he said after he finished the call.

'Come down to the station in the next few days and we'll get it sorted. The forensics mob are coming from Kalgoorlie with the detectives so it's officially a big fucking deal now. I saw the needle in his arm same as you, this is some junkie shitbag, probably running from the law in Perth, he's pulled up in the scrub for a hit, done too much and died. End of fucking story, no great loss to society but procedure and all that means we're gonna make a big deal out of it.'

I agreed with his assessment of the situation. In my time working at the roadhouse I had seen all kinds of dubious characters driving east to west or vice-versa, often running from the law, their families or their lives in general, an endless procession of driftwood. Our dead guy was most likely one of those and would not be missed too much.

Driving back to Madura I thought about our dead guy. How long had he been out there? Who was he? How is it possible in a modern first world country like Australia that someone can die, their body can rot and no one knows or cares about it? Was there someone out there still waiting to hear from him? Hoping that he would ring or email or contact soon?

I got back to Madura and life went on as normal. The story of what I'd found circulated up and down the highway and I got a few questions about it from our regular truckies. After five days I got a call from Dicky Knee telling me to come down to Eucla and make my statement. As I drove along the stretch of highway between us I passed the little dirt track where I had found our dead guy. The officers from Kalgoorlie had worn it a bit more with their comings and goings but it was still barely visible from the highway. No wonder no one had found him until I came along.

I arrived at the Eucla police station, a brand new multi-million dollar monstrosity built because our state Nationals MP was very good at pork barrelling. Dicky Knee was sat at his desk deliberately ignoring the ringing phone.

'Here he is! The man who finds work for me! Ha Ha! No worries mate, grab a seat and we'll get this shit sorted and out of the way. The forensics mob from Kal have done their secret magic bullshit and ruled it suicide, so we're gonna wrap it up without much fuss, just need your statement now.' He was jovial and shared his good mood loudly while he motioned for me to grab a chair and organized a pen and paper. I wrote down the simple truth of what had happened and what I'd found and signed off on it within about ten minutes. Dicky Knee was still cheerful so I took a risk and asked him about the dead man.

He was happy to elaborate on the tale of woe. The man's name was Christopher Major, born and raised in Geraldton, family was fairly poor and more than a little fractured. A father who'd done the bolt with a younger woman leaving the kids with an alcoholic mother, fairly predictable life story after that, trouble at school, a few juvenile arrests and then marginal employment prospects as an adult. A couple of short stints in prison as a man for piddling stuff but an on and off again heroin habit kept him from getting his life together.

A thought occurred to me and I interrupted the story to ask why they were sure it was suicide and not just an ordinary overdose.

'That notebook on the passenger seat? Well he'd written an epic suicide note in that before he died. Fourteen pages long! Can you believe that? What's there to write in a suicide note? 'I'm a dropkick, can't hack it, goodbye' and there you go, done. Don't see why he needed to write fourteen fucking pages.' I was tempted to ask if I could read his note but it was probably too ghoulish and would get me marked out as a weirdo in his book.

'He even had a CD in the car stereo, Pink Floyd, the 'Animals' album. At least he had good taste in music even if he was a dropkick.' I nodded assent. We talked shit for a little while longer about the various Muppets who worked at the roadhouse and dodgy truckies on the highway before I made my excuses and left.

I drove home to Madura in a quietly agitated state. The life story of our dead man niggled at me and refused to leave me in peace. I drove past the spot where I had found him and that bothered me. I got home in a foul mood and shut myself in my room. Sitting there alone, I thought about having a wank to ease off the tension and moodiness, I started up my computer with the intention of finding porn but I thought about the Pink Floyd CD in his car, the album he'd chosen to listen to as he died. I decided I had to find it.

It took me all of about five minutes to find the CD and order it but I spent a solid hour reading the reviews and backstory of this album. From what I could see nearly everyone agreed it was a cracking good album, not as good as their better known masterpieces but still better than nearly everything on the radio today. Why had Christopher Major chosen to die with this '70s dinosaur rock album playing? Why had he chosen to drive all the way out here to the Nullarbor and find a hidden patch of scrub out of sight of everyone to die in? Wouldn't it have been easier to commit suicide back home in Geraldton? If you've made up your mind to die why would you care where it happens? The questions bothered me and not having answers bothered me even more. I had this gnawing feeling that there was something important about his choices, but I couldn't articulate what.

I did some searching online over the next few days and found out that his body had been released by the cops and claimed by his mother in Geraldton. He was cremated and his ashes scattered off the beach at Drummond Cove, a small beachside town that must have had some significance to him. Aside from that it was as though he never existed, so miniscule was his mark on this world. I found it a deeply troubling notion that a man could kill himself, not be found for years and when he was found it was discovered that no one really cared anyway. A person, a life, wiped clean from the Earth with no trace.

Over the next few weeks I ran this notion around my head endlessly. I began to ask troubling questions about my own life and how quickly I would be completely forgotten after I died. I mentally crafted my life story into an obituary and was depressed by how pathetic it sounded. I had bummed around in high school, worked at a supermarket for a while, worked at a bottleshop for a couple of years, joined the army but got discharged on a medical, spent some time working at a mining camp in the NT and eventually ended up here…at a roadhouse on the Nullarbor in exactly the middle of nowhere. It was hardly an inspiring story and I got more depressed as I thought about it. I wondered if our dead guy, Christopher Major of Geraldton, had thought like this before he came out here for his heroin and Pink Floyd-fueled exit.

I was at this low point when the mail arrived and my CD copy of Pink Floyd's 'Animals' album was delivered. I put it on in my room and listened to it the whole way through without pausing. It was good, no denying that, everything that made '70s stadium rock so awesome was represented here, the epic guitar solos, the deep, stoner lyrics, it was pretty damn good. Was it the music I would want to listen to as I died? Not sure.

I was seized with the idea of re-creating the circumstances our man chose to die in, so I took my new CD, my car and headed off towards Mundrabilla. I found the track and headed down to the spot where I had found him. It didn't take me long. I parked my car exactly where his had been before the forensics officers from Kalgoorlie had removed it. Stopping the engine I sat and listened to the wind howling westwards over the saltbush plain. It was sobering to think how alone I was out here, the Nullarbor has a way of forcing you to realize your own isolation; it strips you of the frivolous accessories of civilization and leaves you naked with your life.

I put the CD on and listened as Pink Floyd filled the car and half silenced the wind outside. I let each song play out full to the end with no interruption, some crows flew past but aside from that I may as well have been the only living creature in the world. The CD finished and I turned the stereo off before it could start again. That haunting paranoia of being watched hit me again, but I knew I was alone out here so I sat tight and let the feeling pass.

Feeling rather lost and clueless I started the car and followed the track back out onto the highway. I turned west and headed back to Madura. I was none the wiser about the whole thing.

GRANDPA BOB

They don't make men like Grandpa Bob anymore. At least that's what everyone said at his funeral. Even now all these years later when his name comes up at family gatherings the response of choice is nearly always to remark that they don't make men like him anymore. It's possible that the people who say this actually mean it and it certainly has a strong element of truth but mostly I think they struggle to think of something else to say. You're not supposed to speak ill of the dead and even the people who liked Grandpa Bob would be forced to admit he was a bit of a rogue.

I am one of the few in our family who thought well of Grandpa Bob and I would like to tell his story here. He wasn't famous, rich or talented so this is likely to be the only biography he ever gets. Perhaps it is sad that his entire life will be summed up here in my little story, but if you think about it, the majority of people don't even get that.

Grandpa Bob was born in 1933 in a little place called Boddington in WA. If you go to Boddington now it seems like a go ahead little town, there is a mine up in the hills providing employment and plenty of cashed up retirees have moved there from Perth to spend their twilight years in gardens. Back in 1933 it was the arsehole of nowhere. The local people were dirt poor already and the Depression didn't help matters. The only reason most people back then didn't starve was because every house had a veggie patch and some chooks. When they literally didn't have a penny to buy food they could always go out the back, dig up some spuds and carrots and get a few eggs. It wasn't much but it kept body and soul together.

Grandpa Bob's family were getting by, his father had semi-regular work as a fencing contractor and they had the standard veggie patch and chooks out the back. It wasn't so much the financial situation that blighted his young life but the spiritual one. His father was a fundamentalist and belonged to some obscure Protestant sect which no longer exists. The type of religion determined to make this life a misery so that the next life can be bliss. Basically everything fun was forbidden and the followers of this group were encouraged to have a grim attitude to life and to spread this grim attitude to others for their own good.

From what I understand Grandpa Bob rebelled against this faith from his very early years. This rebellion was met with savage beatings from his father which only ended when Grandpa Bob grew up and started hitting back. The story I've heard from now deceased family members is that Grandpa Bob had a growth spurt as teenage boys often do and felt his increased size exempted him from taking hidings. His father disagreed. It all came to a head one day and Grandpa Bob beat his father so savagely he thought he had killed him.

Bob did a runner to Perth thinking the law was right behind him. His father hadn't died but was sore and bitter. He vowed his son would never set foot in his home again and he never did.

Grandpa Bob had got to Perth and kept checking the newspaper to see if his father had been reported murdered. A week went past and there was nothing. He realised he hadn't killed him but that he could never go home again.

He wasn't actually sorry.

Now came the question of what to do? He started looking for a job in Perth when he saw the recruitment posters. The Korean War had just started and the army were taking any fit young lad who applied. Grandpa Bob thought about it for maybe five seconds. He was strong from working out bush, he knew how to shoot and the discipline of the army couldn't actually be worse than the discipline of his father. He went in the little office and signed up.

You've got to remember that Grandpa Bob was a total country hick. He'd never been further than Perth in his life, he didn't have a passport and wouldn't have known how to get one and he'd probably never seen an Asian person in his life up to that point. I'm pretty sure he didn't even know where Korea was when he signed up to go fight there. The army didn't care; he was fit, could shoot straight and mostly did what he was told. That was enough.

After training, his battalion shipped out to Korea. To say it was a culture shock is an understatement. It was his first and only time outside of Australia. His upbringing in a tiny bush town with daily doses of Christian fundamentalist dogma gave him no frame of reference for understanding the Korean people.

When I was a young boy and Grandpa Bob was an old man he used to get me to fetch him a whiskey or two and as a sort of reward he would tell me stories about the war. The more whiskeys I fetched him the better the stories would become. I believe that these stories were at least mostly true. I think the whiskey diminished his capacity for bullshit, in vino veritas and all that.

He told me about seeing snow in Korea. The first and only time in his life he ever saw snow. He told me about how his section was crawling across a frozen rice paddy when the Chinese started mortaring them. Fortunately the mortars punched through the thin layer of ice and exploded in the slush below, dampening their effect and almost certainly saving his life.

He told me about crawling over no-man's land in the dark to attack Chinese positions. He told me about bayonetting a Chinese soldier in the face by the light of a flare. He told me about getting leave for a few days behind the lines and going to a brothel. His mates had pegged him as a totally clueless bumpkin and told him that the pussies of Asian girls actually went horizontally side to side like their eyes. He believed them because he didn't know any better. When he got his girl undressed in the room and saw her pussy was not really any different from the white women he'd had in Australia he went to the Mama San and complained. His mates had thought it hilarious and gave him shit about it for a long time after.

Eventually as he told these tales the whiskey would take effect and he would get sleepy. He'd shoo me off and tell me to go play with my cousins. I would think about these yarns for a long time. To my young mind Grandpa Bob seemed like the greatest adventurer of all time.

When he got back from Korea he got an honourable discharge from the army. Back in those days when you left the army after doing your time they gave you a couple weeks pay and a bus ticket back to the place you'd enlisted from. That was it. Grandpa Bob found himself back in Perth not really any better off than when he'd joined the army a couple of years earlier.

All he had ever known up to that point was farm work and soldiering. Since the soldiering had come to an end the obvious thing to do was go find some farm work. He hit the road and within a week was working for an embittered old cocky on his place just outside Moora.

Now I don't want to be one of those people who harps on about the past being better than the present, but in this case it was. In those times a man who had a bit of muscle and half a brain could find himself a job without too much bother and earn enough money to hold his head up with pride. Grandpa Bob had barely more than a sixth grade education and no certificates for his many skills but he could walk into a job on a farm and earn his bread like a man.

Over the next few years Grandpa Bob travelled around the wheat and sheep country of WA working at odd jobs, mostly on farms but occasionally in the little towns that dotted the plain. One of my cousins tried to do the family history and used modern software to try and track where he'd been for these years. It was almost impossible as he was never registered to vote, doesn't appear to have lodged tax returns or filled out census forms anywhere. What she did find was a couple of run-ins with the law in various little towns, mostly for drunken nonsense, and apparently he was almost murdered by an irate father of a pregnant girl.

The incident happened in Tammin which is a tiny place even today but in 1955 must have been the real backwoods of the state. Apparently the girl was barely above the legal age of consent at the time and had confessed in tears to her parents that she was pregnant. She named Grandpa Bob as the father of her unborn child. He had been working at the railway siding in town for a few months.

The girl's father apparently marched down to the railway workers camp gun in hand and took a pot shot at Bob as he was making a cup of tea in the camp kitchen. The urn was peppered with shotgun pellets but no harm was done although Bob wisely left town right away. The local constabulary arrested the man and let him cool down in the cells overnight. They declined to press charges and the girl was sent to a home for unwed mothers run by the Salvation Army. Her baby was born and adopted out. As far as I know, Grandpa Bob never saw the girl or her child again.

My cousin who discovered this when she was attempting to do the family history got curious and tried to find the woman and her child. She got her name from the Police records and began her search. Unfortunately the woman had died by the time she tracked her down. Apparently she came back to Tammin from the home for unwed mothers after having the baby and never left the town again. She is buried in the local cemetery. Her baby was adopted out by the Salvation Army and grew up in a nice middle class Christian home in Perth. She became a nurse as an adult and had children of her own with her husband. We were going to contact her to talk about our shared genetic history but there was no indication that she knew about being adopted or cared about her biological parents so we thought it best to let sleeping dogs lie.

It is worth noting that when my cousin tried to track his movements through the state between the years 1953 and 1957 the only thing she could find was this incident. He evidently lived in the margins of society. Shearer's quarters, railway camps and occasionally sleeping rough as he went from job to job and town to town. That sort of life doesn't leave much trace.

In 1957 he was working on a farm just outside the tiny town of Three Springs. It was here that he met his wife Caroline, my grandmother. Apparently her mother, my great-grandmother, owned and ran a little tea shop in the town. I know the sort of place, they still had them in every country town when I was young, charming little joints that served Devonshire teas and scones with jam and cream. All the women of the town would go there for a cuppa and the latest gossip.

For whatever reason, one day in 1957 Grandpa Bob decided to forgo the pub and have some scones with jam and cream. He was served by Caroline and was keen on her from day one. I don't know the full story of their courtship only that within six months they got married in the Three Springs Anglican church. They moved to Geraldton shortly after where Grandpa Bob attempted to settle down and be a family man.

Caroline was kept busy having babies; between their marriage in 1957 and his abandonment of her in 1971 she'd had eight children and one miscarriage. A large number even back then. Grandpa Bob was one of those old fashioned blokes to whom it never occurred that women were for anything other than domesticity and breeding. If you had asked him what Caroline's hopes and dreams were he would have looked at you like you were a bit odd. It wouldn't be accurate to say he was a misogynist, he didn't hate women, he just thought they had a very set and limited role in life.

Whatever Caroline's hopes and dreams had been before marriage the reality of being a perpetually pregnant housewife soon crushed them. Then the affairs started. My cousin who did the research found at least two bastard children fathered by Grandpa Bob while he was married to Caroline. Both of the women were barmaids at local pubs and both went off to homes for unwed mothers. Perhaps Grandpa Bob should have got commission.

My cousin found one of these women through a website for relinquishing mothers trying to find the children they'd adopted out. We met her one day in Perth to ask her about Grandpa Bob. Her story was simple enough, young girl working her first job at the pub, Bob gives her a bit of chat and the occasional lift home, one thing leads to another and she was in a home for unwed mothers. Her story does have a happy(ish) ending though, she made contact with the child she gave up for adoption years later and they have a good relationship now.

The role of responsible family man never fit very well for Grandpa Bob and in 1971 he decided he'd had jack of it. He told Caroline he'd had enough and packed a swag and left. Just like that.

Interestingly he left no record whatsoever of where he went from 1971 until 1976. The record is completely blank. It's like he walked off the edge of the world for five years. When asked about it years later, he would always get uncomfortable and mumble something about going 'up north' or 'out bush' but never more than that.

My theory is he went to the NT or somewhere equally remote for five years and thought about his life while hiding out and not participating in society. My cousin thinks he was up to something highly illegal, maybe drug smuggling or something similar and hid it well enough to never get caught.

I personally favour my theory and I think I have some evidence for it. When I was maybe nine years old we were sitting around watching TV one evening and the ABC had a doco on about Gough Whitlam and the dismissal. Grandpa Bob struggled to follow it and kept asking questions about who the people were, he didn't seem to know who John Kerr was nor did he have any idea who Gough Whitlam was. This would fit with my theory of his being somewhere really remote for the years between 1971 and 1976. Remember that before the age of the internet and satellite TV, if you went somewhere like Arnhem Land or the Tanami Desert you basically fell of the edge of the world. It's entirely possible, and I think probable, that Grandpa Bob completely missed the Whitlam years.

Wherever he went and whatever he did in those years, he took it to the grave. We still have no proof of his existence for those five years. When he does emerge again in the historical record he was living in Port Lincoln in early 1977. The wife he had abandoned back in WA had sorted out a divorce so he was free to marry another local barmaid who caught his eye.

Her name was Annette and they were married at the registry office in Port Lincoln. She was already in the family way and gave birth later that year. Grandpa Bob was working for a local trucking company that mostly moved grain and livestock for the farmers in the district. He seems to have handled this second attempt at being a family man much better than his first try. As far as we know there were no affairs or other impregnated barmaids. He had four children with Annette and lived a fairly quiet life, although he started to drink a little more than he previously had.

As is the way of men he got older, grumpier and fatter. He drank more and participated in life a bit less. He seemed to be worn out from it all. As the 1980s rolled around his children from his first marriage were mostly grown up and started to find their own way in life. Some of them had families of their own. The levels of bitterness amongst them varied, some willing to forgive and forget Grandpa Bob's abandonment of them and their mother, while others wished him dead.

My mother was willing to give reconciliation a try and I was taken to visit Grandpa Bob frequently as a kid. These are some happy memories and I treasure them to this day. I remember running around in the yard with my cousins. I remember the stories Grandpa Bob used to tell.

He died in 1989 when I was still just a boy. The whiskey and cigarettes did him in the end. He wasn't a rich man and left no great estate for his family. His obituary in the Port Lincoln paper mentioned his service in the Korean War and his many children without going into much detail.

I can't help but feel that he deserves more than that, which is why I've written this story. He lived a wild life and was no saint, that much is true; but he was his own man. He never bludged a cent off anyone but earned his bread with sweat. He endured poverty, hardship and war without complaint.

They will never make a statue of him or give him a page in the history books, but his real legacy is us lot. Thanks to his way with women I am related to half of Australia. Not the good half mind you, the country bumpkin white trash half, but still' it pleases me to think I have the genes of a strong man who made his own way in the world and lived on his own terms. When I have children of my own I will tell them about Grandpa Bob and if I'm honest, I hope to see something of him in them.

ABOUT THE AUTHOR

Lewis Woolston grew up in a small beach bum town in Western Australia. He hated it and left as soon as he could.

He misspent most of his youth in Perth and Adelaide, did a short and miserable stint in the Army, then spent years living and working on remote roadhouses on the Nullarbor and in the Northern Territory.

He lives in Alice Springs with his wife and daughter.

ACKNOWLEDGEMENTS

Thanks to *Flycatcher* for originally publishing 'A Row of Bottlebrush Trees' and 'Postcard from Cairns', and thanks to *Tulpa* for originally publishing 'The Family Farm'.

The author would also like to thank Helen Travers who was the first person to see most of these stories and was always encouraging.

ABOUT TRUTH SERUM PRESS

Established in 2014, Truth Serum Press is based in Adelaide, Australia, but publishes books from authors in all parts of the English-speaking world.

Like sister presses Pure Slush Books and Everytime Press, Truth Serum Press is part of the Bequem Publishing collective.

Truth Serum Press publishes novels, novellas, and short story collections. We no longer publish single author poetry anthologies.

Sometimes, when the mood strikes us, we publish multi-author anthologies. Generally, we publish fiction … and sometimes (just sometimes) we publish non-fiction.

We publish in English, and we would gladly publish in other languages if we understood them.

We like books that take us to new places, to new experiences and inside new minds and hearts.

We also like to laugh.

If you think we might like your novel or novella or short story collection, contact us at truthserumpress@live.com.au.

Visit our website at https://truthserumpress.net/.

Also from TRUTH SERUM PRESS

https://truthserumpress.net/catalogue/

  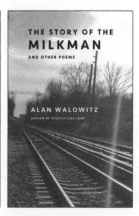

- *Easy Money and Other Stories* by Steve Evans
  978-1-925536-81-2 (paperback) 978-1-925536-82-9 (eBook)
- *Minotaur and Other Stories* by Salvatore Difalco
  978-1-925536-79-9 (paperback) 978-1-925536-80-5 (eBook)
- *The Story of the Milkman* by Alan Walowitz
  978-1-925536-76-8 (paperback) 978-1-925536-77-5 (eBook)

- *The Book of Acrostics* by John Lambremont, Sr.
  978-1-925536-52-2 (paperback) 978-1-925536-53-9 (eBook)
- *Square Pegs* by Rob Walker
  978-1-925536-62-1 (paperback) 978-1-925536-63-8 (eBook)
- *Cheat Sheets* by Edward O'Dwyer
  978-1-925536-60-7 (paperback) 978-1-925536-61-4 (eBook)

Also from TRUTH SERUM PRESS

https://truthserumpress.net/catalogue/

 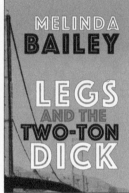 

- *The Crazed Wind* by Nod Ghosh
  978-1-925536-58-4 (paperback) 978-1-925536-59-1 (eBook)
- *Legs and the Two-Ton Dick* by Melinda Bailey
  978-1-925536-37-9 (paperback) 978-1-925536-38-6 (eBook)
- *Dollhouse Masquerade* by Samuel E. Cole
  978-1-925536-43-0 (paperback) 978-1-925536-44-7 (eBook)

- *Kiss Kiss* by Paul Beckman
  978-1-925536-21-8 (paperback) 978-1-925536-22-5 (eBook)
- *Inklings* by Irene Buckler
  978-1-925536-41-6 (paperback) 978-1-925536-42-3 (eBook)
- *On the Bitch* by Matt Potter
  978-1-925536-45-4 (paperback) 978-1-925536-46-1 (eBook)

Also from TRUTH SERUM PRESS

https://truthserumpress.net/catalogue/

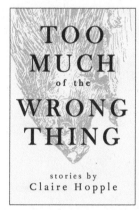  

- *Too Much of the Wrong Thing* by Claire Hopple
  978-1-925536-33-1 (paperback) 978-1-925536-34-8 (eBook)
- *Track Tales* by Mercedes Webb-Pullman
  978-1-925536-35-5 (paperback) 978-1-925536-36-2 (eBook)
- *Luck and Other Truths* by Richard Mark Glover
  978-1-925101-77-5 (paperback) 978-1-925536-04-1 (eBook)

  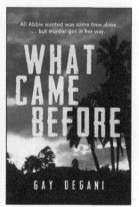

- *Hello Berlin!* by Jason S. Andrews
  978-1-925536-11-9 (paperback) 978-1-925536-12-6 (eBook)
- *Deer Michigan* by Jack C. Buck
  978-1-925536-25-6 (paperback) 978-1-925536-26-3 (eBook)
- *What Came Before* by Gay Degani
  978-1-925536-05-8 (paperback) 978-1-925536-06-5 (eBook)

Also from TRUTH SERUM PRESS

https://truthserumpress.net/catalogue/

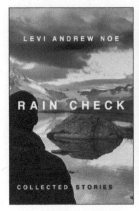  

- *Rain Check* by Levi Andrew Noe
  978-1-925536-09-6 (paperback) 978-1-925536-10-2 (eBook)
- *Based on True Stories* by Matt Potter
  978-1-925101-75-1 (paperback) 978-1-925101-76-8 (eBook)
- *The Miracle of Small Things* by Guilie Castillo Oriard
  978-1-925101-73-7 (paperback) 978-1-925101-74-4 (eBook)

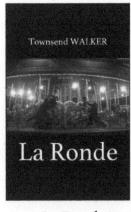 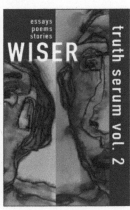 

- *La Ronde* by Townsend Walker
  978-1-925101-64-5 (paperback) 978-1-925101-65-2 (eBook)
- *Wiser Truth Serum Vol. #2*
  978-1-925536-31-7 (paperback) 978-1-925536-32-4 (eBook)
- *True Truth Serum Vol. #1*
  978-1-925536-29-4 (paperback) 978-1-925536-30-0 (eBook)